Carrie - You've been a very BAD girl

by Nicole Ferguson

Carrie - You've been a very BAD girl

Nicole Ferguson

ISBN 978-1625122124

Published by

Tutor Turtle Press, LLC

1027 S. Pendleton St., Suite B-10

Easley, SC 29642

TABLE OF CONTENTS

Chapter One

"I can't even tell you how fantastic your ass looks in that dress."

Shocked I turned to see who had made such a comment to me. I wasn't used to hearing such things and the comment alone shocked me. Behind me stood a guy in a fancy suit with a broad grin on his face. I was at the wedding of one of my father's friends. My father was acting as pastor for the wedding and I had been invited out of respect. I was surprised actually since I hadn't seen my father in about a month. Being the pastor's daughter had never made my life easier and recently I had left his flock to venture out in the world to see what he was afraid of me seeing. I wanted to live after all. I felt like I had been suffocating my whole life and I was only 18. My father was often strict and overbearing. I didn't like being around it all anymore.

Since being away from my father I had lost my virginity and slept with a few other men as well. He would be so disappointed in me but call it acting out if you will, but I needed to experience these things that my father was so determined to deny me. My father never let me have any fun and I was sick of it. So maybe I shouldn't have slept with three men in one month but I was desperate to prove my father wrong, that fun stuff wasn't all bad. Plus I really enjoyed being with those guys and so far I saw no reason to return back to my father's flock.

Looking at this guy I had to wonder how he managed to approached girls so confidently and say the most outrageous things. He was so handsome too, wasn't that just my luck? I had realized through my limited time in the dating world that most hot guys turned out to be dicks. So far this guy was living up to that theory perfectly. Two of the three guys I had slept with hadn't even bothered to call me the next day and they were ridiculously hot, so this guy wasn't about to woe me over any time soon. The one average looking guy that I had dated had worshipped the ground that I walked on.

Not that I had any musings that this guy would be interested in anything more than a good lay. He was probably just like all the others. He was horny for sex and nothing else. I looked him over and admired his athletic build. He had beautiful green eyes and sandy blonde hair. He looked like he could charm me into the sack no problem. But I wasn't about to let him do that.

"What did you say?" I wasn't expecting an apology. Guys like that never thought they did anything wrong. It was actually sort of irritating. It was best to just ignore him.

"Oh, I just wanted you to know that you have one hell of an ass. That dress looks dynamite on you and it hugs your ass nicely."

I chuckled, taken aback. This guy was a real piece of work. His comments were so out there and obviously sexual. Did he really think that it was okay to talk to a lady that way? My father may be a lot of things but he still taught me that a man should respect a woman at all times.

Did this really work on other girls? There was no doubt the guy probably dated a lot. He was really hot, in a Ryan Reynolds sort of way.

"I'm sorry but do you really think talking like that to me is going to work in your favor?"

He smiled, "You mean it's not?" I couldn't believe the guy was actually enjoying my discomfort. He moved closer to me and I was stunned when I noticed my heart beating faster. It couldn't be possible, not with him? He was right in my personal space and instead of it making me uncomfortable I found myself getting a bit turned on by his forcefulness.

"There are some girls that like a man that they can try to tame. Are you one of those girls?"

I laughed, feeling like a total idiot for even talking to him. "You have to be joking? That sounds like a lot of work to me. No thank you."

"Comeon, you can't tell me you are the least bit interested in me."

I could not even believe what I was hearing. This guy was live in front of me and I was starting to wonder if I was the target of some kind of prank.

I started shaking my head because there were not even any more words I could say to him.

"Nope," I muttered.

"Comeon, it's rare I get to meet a girl with an ass that I could kiss."

I gasped as I blushed deeply. The guy really knew how to make a girl feel heady.

"I guarantee beautiful, that if you want to play with me I won't leave you with any regrets." He was right beside my ear, his voice breathy, and warm against my ear. Chills ran up my spine and I could barely catch my own breath as he talked. What the hell was wrong with me? I couldn't even believe I was responding to him in this way. But there was just something about him that made me want.

"Look, I've heard all about guys like you. You come to a wedding and you try to score with women. Is this a weekly thing for you?"

He chuckled, his eyes still fixed on me. I couldn't deny that I liked the look in his eyes. There was something about the way a guy looked at you, like you were the best thing he would taste all day. I liked when a man looked at me that way. It was a pretty big turn on for me. He stepped towards me and I stepped back trying to keep him out of my personal space. I didn't trust him in the least. It didn't faze him one bit however, in fact it just made him smile wider.

"Tell me you aren't the least bit curious to find out what it would be like for me to devour you. I like to take my time."

Devour? I had never heard a guy talk about sex in that manner.

"Believe me, I don't need to know. You want to sleep with me and then I'll never hear from you again. Am I getting close?"

He chuckled again, "you are pretty feisty aren't you. And no it's not a slam bam thank you mam thing with me. I like to take my time with a woman. I even like to come back for seconds."

I was no longer sure if we were still talking about sex or if it had moved on to food at that point.

"Plus, you seem to be neglected."

I laughed, "Excuse me? And what makes you think that."

"Well you aren't here with anyone are you?"

"I don't have to be, I'm an independent woman. You have heard of those, haven't you?"

"Oh sure but you aren't talking to anyone."

"I don't have to be, I'm just casually mingling. You are the one that's already pre-drinking before the ceremony even starts."

We both looked down at the drink he held in his hand. He looked momentarily sheepish but it didn't last long.

"I'm just celebrating at a wedding my dear."

"Of course you are. You should be pretty drunk by dinner then."

"I'll have you know my body can consume a lot of alcohol before it gets tipsy."

"Now don't you sound like a real keeper?"

He wasted no time in moving close to me and I wondered if he even knew what personal space was. He cupped my chin and I thought for a moment that he was going to kiss me. Would I stop him, I wasn't too sure. He didn't however and when his hand left my chin it tingled as if he still held it. My throat had gone dry and I doubted I could form a sentence even if I wanted to.

"You really are stunning you know."

I had no words. In my limited dating experience no guy had ever talked to me that way. I couldn't even believe what I was hearing. I had never had a guy refer to me as stunning before; pretty, sure but never stunning. My whole body was warming up to his closeness but I refused to be taken in by him. He was trouble there was no doubt in my mind that he was. I couldn't figure out his game plan, aside from trying to sleep with me. There were plenty of beautiful and eligible females at the wedding. Why was he with me when he could have anyone else in the room? I couldn't understand why he was wasting any of his time with me. What was worse was we shared an undeniable chemistry together and that was the last thing I could understand. Why was I feeling any kind of attraction to this guy? It just didn't make any sense to me.

 His hand moved to the small of my back and grew warm there.

"I think you and I would really be hot together and I would really like to show you that." He was whispering in my ear while his hand travelled down to my ass and squeezed it.

"What the hell?" I said as I pushed him away. Knocking his arm I watched in horror as his drink spilled down the front of me.

"Oh shit. I'm so sorry."

 I looked down the front of my dress feeling like crying at the sight of the stain on it.

10

Chapter Two

"You asshole!"

We were both grabbing at napkins on the flimsy hope that I could get the stain out of my dress. Why did I continue to wear light colors to events like this? It was just asking for trouble. I should have worn black, and then I wouldn't have this problem. He started dabbing at my breasts and irritated I snatched the napkins out of his head.

"What the hell do you think you are doing? Stop trying to cop a feel? You already ruined my dress."

He laughed which made me want to kill him that much more.

"Oh is this funny to you?" I hissed at him.

He stopped laughing, "No of course not. I just laughed because you insinuated I was trying to feel you up. Look, I feel really bad about your dress. I'm so sorry."

"Oh really? Well I have a wedding to attend in a few minutes and my dress looks like it belongs in the trash. So thank you for that. All you are doing is driving me insane."

"Tell me that`s not a good thing?"

"Oh my god, will you seriously just leave me alone?"

He grabbed a hold of my hand as I looked up at him from the mess of my dress.

"Hey seriously, I was only trying to make light of the situation. I'm really not a jerk. Trust me."

"Oh sure. I bet. It must be totally normal for you to grab some girls' ass you don't know at a wedding. If you hadn't been feeling me up my dress wouldn't look like this."

"I guess I thought you might like it."

I shook my head slowly. I couldn't even believe what I was witnessing. This behavior had to have worked for him before in order for him to be so confident with himself. He was truly a piece of work and I had no idea where something like him had come from. He was hot as hell, there was no doubt about that, but every time he opened his mouth I was left amazed, and not in a good way. Plus there was still this crazy chemistry thing we had between us that was truly unexplainable. I should want to tear him to pieces and yet I liked it every time he got close to me.

He was smiling down at me and I wondered where he got all his confidence from, I certainly was never that self-assured. I would never be able to speak to a guy as easily as he spoke to me. What was truly amazing to me was that he wasn't fazed at all by the fact that I wanted him to get away from me and as quickly as possible.

To my surprise he slowly brushed my hair behind my ear which cause chills to go up my spine again. My breathing was becoming labored and my heart beat harder in my chest. I knew that I should tell him to fuck off but I really couldn't bring myself to do so. I should be worrying about my dress but I was having a hard time worrying about anything but him in that moment. He totally possessed me with such little effort and that pissed me off more than anything. I was overwhelmed with his presence, the fact that he was so close to me. I would not be able to think straight as long as he was so close to me so I pushed him away from me.

"Will you back off for a moment? What is wrong with you, or do you even know? Look at my dress! How am I supposed to go in there looking like this?"

The look on his face caused me to frown. "What?"

He smiled, "You have a fire in you that I find incredibly attractive. I almost want to irritate you more just to see what you might do to me. Do you bite in the bedroom?"

My mouth dropped to the ground.

"Relax! Let me take you to that bathroom, we will get that stain out for you, even if I have to lick it out myself."

I started laughing, mainly because I didn't know what else to do. Suddenly he grabbed my hand and led me through the crowd of people waiting for the ceremony to start. My father would kill me if he saw me enter the ceremony with a stain all over my dress. He would blame it on the fact that I left home to live on my own. He also wouldn't be happy to see me with a man who was leading me around by the hand. He would assume we were together and I wouldn't hear the end of it. There I was being led around by some guy that had some kind of sexual manipulation that worked perfectly on me.

I followed him down a hallway praying to God that I would not be noticed by anyone. I watched as people started to come into the building and make their way into the ceremony. I had to move fast or I wasn't going to be there on time. We finally found the ladies room and he pushed the door open and pulled me into the room after him.

"Ahh, correct me if I'm wrong but I don't think you belong in here. What if someone sees you in here? My father would have a complete fit and believe me I don't need that in my life right now." I pulled my hand from his trying to look as angry as possible. The warmth of his hand still lingered on mine. Despite my protests I kind of liked it when he held my hand.

Gosh Carrie, you really are losing your mind. This guy turns you on? Really? Wow, you can sure pick them.

I sighed deeply trying to concentrate. I should have demanded he wait outside. I could handle my dress on my own. I was confident of it. Instead, I watched in silence as he tested the tap water. He rolled out some of the paper towel in the machine and then wet it. Looking down at my dress I could at least be thankful he hadn't used Cola in his drink.

He came to me and started dabbing my dress lightly. I'm not sure what was going to be worse, the stain that I had or the wet spot that would be left after we cleaned the dress up. I looked at him with relief as I saw the stain slowly disappearing.

"Oh thank God, it's actually going away."

"See, didn't I say it wasn't that bad? You did kind of treat me like I was the devil."

"Aren't you?"

"Okay, maybe I should be thankful I was able to save your dress at least. I think it won't take long for the wet spot to disappear either."

"Well it's still pretty noticeable."

He looked around the bathroom and then a smile appeared on his face.

"I have an idea. Come here."

I walked over to the dryers attached to the wall and I smiled at his brilliance.

"Well this is something at least. Thank you."

I stood in front of the dryer and pressed the button as hot air spilled on me. I watched as the wet spot slowly dried before my eyes.

"Oh thank god, it's working I can't believe this."

"Well you're welcome. Glad I could help."

Suddenly he was right behind me and I gasped. My breath caught as he moved right up against my butt. He lowered himself so that his mouth was close to my ear.

"I don't know what it is about you but I have a hard time not being close to you. It's like I have to be right next to you."

I felt warm all over and my eyes closed. In that moment I wanted him to devour me. He was right. There was something about him that ignited something in me when he was close. It was like it was natural for him to be near me, as if it was meant to be. I had never felt like that around anyone before and the fact that I felt it around him confused me. I started to feel a little dizzy when he pushed himself into me. His hands found my ass once again and he squeezed them gently. "You have such a firm little ass."

He was so fixated on that part of my body. His hands on my ass warmed me through my dress. I didn't know what was happening to my body at that moment. One minute I was pissed that his hands were on my ass yet again and the next I felt a need inside me for him. I could barely concentrate on where I was and who I was with. The sensation of his hands on my ass was driving me a little crazy. Suddenly I felt wet between my legs and that amazed me even more. Was he actually turning me on right now? I couldn't even believe what was happening. I must be losing my mind, I had to be. There was no doubt about the throb I was feeling between my legs.

I have to stop this right now. I can't do this. It's insane. It's insane for me to feel anything at all for this man. ESPECIALLY this man! God, he was everything I didn't want in a boyfriend. Well maybe that wasn't entirely true. He was ridiculously hot. It never hurt to have a hot boyfriend especially if this was what it felt like to have him touch you.

I turned around suddenly noticing immediately the feeling of his hands no longer being on my ass anymore. It was not a good feeling. He pulled me away from the dryer and pushed me against the wall.

"I don't think this is a good idea. It's confusing and you're kind of an idiot."

He smiled before he claimed my mouth beneath his. If I thought the heat was consuming before I absolutely lit up when he kissed me. He tasted sweet and his mouth was warm. I couldn't help myself I kissed him back as passionately as I could. I needed to match his intensity. I had never felt like this before in my life. No man had ever kissed me that way or brought out such an intense chemistry in me. I was out of breath from his kisses and I was beginning to feel overwhelmed again. I pushed against his chest and he relented.

"What's wrong? This feels incredible."

"I can't breathe. It's too much."

He smiled at me and moved close to me yet again. I clearly had no control over the situation and I was beginning to lose the ability to care. I was beginning to want to be consumed. To see what it felt to let him do whatever he wanted to me. Would that be so bad? Would it be bad to let him have his way with me? I didn't know why, there was really no explanation for it but I couldn't remember the last time I had wanted something more than this man. And what made it worse was I wasn't pretty confident I didn't even like him. He drove me nuts in the smallest ways. His arrogance appalled me and the fact that he touched me without even a consideration on whether I wanted him to or not bordered on the absurd.

He softly kissed my mouth again and I inhaled the musky scent of him. His touch was exhilarating as he cupped my chin and bent down for another kiss. The kisses may have started off softly but it wasn't longed before his mouth pressed into mine hard. His hands found their way into my hair and he pulled me in close, so close that I was amazed that they hadn't molded into one body. His tongue slid into my mouth and touched my own. I moaned softly and when he kissed me he took my tongue in his mouth and sucked on it. *God, he's so good at kissing, I can barely keep up.* His kisses were insanely passionate and he nipped and sucked at my lips. I was paralyzed beneath him as my body responded to his kisses in ways I had never felt before. I wasn't sure what was happening to my body, but I was aware that a kiss had never made my panties wet before. But that time...with him I was aching in every area of my body. I needed him and wanted him in every way that mattered.

His hand found my breasts and he cupped the fullness of them. He kneaded my breast causing my nipple to pucker underneath his grasp. I was so incredible horny and I wanted him to take that need away for me.

"You are driving me crazy girl. Your body is incredible and I wish I could see what you looked like without this dress."

Why do I have a wedding to attend to right now? Why? Why now, I need this. I need to feel like this always.

I was shocked by the thoughts that were raging steadfast through my mind. They were taking over my reasoning and moving forward with their own wishes. I had never behaved that way once ever in my life. I was a good girl, I never did anything wrong and I always knew the men I chose to sleep with. Always. Well maybe I hadn't been on my best behavior lately since I left my dad's home but I certainly had never engaged in sex in a bathroom with a stranger. Especially when my father was just in the other room conducting a wedding. I wondered briefly if my father had noticed I was late for the wedding. He may have scanned the room for me and saw that I had yet to arrive.

My lips were consumed once again and all thoughts filtered out of my head. I didn't understand how that man who had done nothing but irritate me from the moment he met me had managed to have me pinned up against the bathroom wall, and yet I had no problem with it at all.

That wasn't entirely true, there was a part of me that knew I should pull myself away from him and run like the wind in the opposite direction. But the dominate part of me was enjoying herself, enjoying having his hands on my body and his tongue exploring my mouth. I molded my lips once again into his and he started to lift my dress up. *My God, was he going to try to have sex with me right then and there? Was I going to let him?*

He grabbed my ass once again underneath my dress that time and I moaned against his lips. It was then that I heard a sound. Sort of like an amplification of someone's voice.

"Wait...hold on one second."

He wasn't listening. His hands still on my ass he was kissing my jawline and then my throat. My eyes fluttered closed again and it was then that I heard it clearly. It was someone talking, a man, and he was obviously talking into a microphone. I recognized the voice but I couldn't quite pinpoint on where I had heard it before. Why would someone be talking right now?

"Oh my god!" I cried out.

That stopped him in his tracks.

"What? What's wrong?"

I pulled away from him and started pulling down my dress.

"The wedding is starting! Can't you hear my dad talking?"

"Shit. You're not the only one who is late." He started straightening out his shirt as well. I made a beeline for the bathroom door.

"Wait! I don't even know your name."

I pulled open the door and without looking back I called out, "Carrie!"

"I'm Jeff," he shouted after me.

I didn't bother to stick around to see what else he had to say. The name Jeff rung around in my head as I made my way into the ceremony. Well at least I knew his name. I opened the door and realized quite plainly that things had indeed got started without me. There was no way I could go in without being noticed. Everyone was already seated. I turned around expecting to see Jeff behind me but he was nowhere to be found. Where had he gone?

Blushing furiously but with my head held high I made my way into the ceremony and took a seat as close to the back as I could to avoid any further embarrassment. I caught my father's look as he glared my way before looking back at the bride and groom.

Oh god, what the hell was wrong with me?

Chapter Three

I avoided my father's glances as much as possible. I knew he was angry with me and it would be another thing on his list to be mad at me about. I scanned the room full of people and gasped when I saw Jeff closer to the front. How had he got in ahead of me? He must have gone in the side door. He smiled at me and all I could do was groan. What was wrong with me? Maybe my father was right about leaving the flock.

Jeff smiled at me with what could definitely be a twinkle in his eyes. I closed my eyes slowly, cursing myself. There was the guy who I had just been dry humping in the bathroom a few moments ago. Oh wouldn't my father be proud. In fact he wouldn't be. He would kill me if he had any idea what I had been doing with Jeff in the bathroom.

I looked over at Jeff again and found he was still watching me intently, like he wanted to eat me up right then and there. He was enjoying himself far too much.

There was no way I was getting myself tangled up with that man again. No way, he was just trouble. I needed to forget that embarrassing bathroom scene and avoid Jeff at all costs.

I could still hear the things he had said to me and the way his body felt pressed up against mine. I still couldn't believe the way he had spoken to me and how much I had liked it.

"You are driving me crazy girl. Your body is incredible and I wish I could see what you looked like without this dress."

I was no virgin but I also didn't have very much experience in the dating world. In fact I might as well be a virgin for all the experience that I had. The ones I had dated were too young to even try speaking that way to me.

Whether I had wanted to admit it or not, I had wanted Jeff, wanted him more than I had wanted any other man in my life. I didn't know why, he was a pig all things considered, and yet I had been drawn to him. He was the kind of guy that would surely break my heart into pieces.

Jeff's hands on my body, they just took whatever they wanted and I kind of liked that. He was very dominating and that was intriguing for someone who had no experience in that way of sex. Jeff had started lifting my dress right there in the bathroom during the ceremony my father was performing…it all seemed so bad.

The more I thought about my bathroom experience the harder it was for me to concentrate on the ceremony. The way Jeff had touched me numbed my brain and made me feel hot all over. He had kissed me with a purpose and that had caused my body to hum against him. What would have happened between us had there been no ceremony to go to? I was caught between feelings of excitement and of being ashamed of what I had done. That was my father's doing however, it was hard to think of having sex without feeling ashamed because of my father. He believed that sex was only meant for a married union and I was nowhere near being married.

What would have happened after he pulled my panties down? I grew warm all over again just thinking about it. Would I have bent over and let him enter me?

"I now pronounce you man and wife...you may kiss the bride!"

The words brought me back to the present. How could I have missed the whole ceremony while daydreaming about Jeff? The couple kissed and there were cheers all around.

I watched the couple leave the church and I looked over at Jeff again. I couldn't see where he had gone and then suddenly someone had grabbed my arm and was leading me along behind him. It was Jeff, how had he got to me so quickly? My arm tingled where he held me. When we got out of the church I pulled my arm from him.

"Hey, what are you doing?"

"I'm not doing this with you. I have to go find my father."

"Come on, I say we go back to the bathroom and finish what we started."

"Are you crazy?'

"Do you need me to take you on a date first?"

"No! God, why are you so irritating? I don't have any interest in dating you. What we did was a mistake."

"Carrie!"

I spun around as my father walked over to me. Oh god, I could not have my father see me with Jeff. I turned to him and said, "Stay away from me."

I headed towards my father so he wouldn't assume I was associated with Jeff. "Daddy hi, the ceremony was wonderful."

"I'm surprised you showed up at all. You were late enough."

"Yeah, sorry about that. I was running late because I got lost." Guilt ran through me. I wasn't sure how my dad made me feel so guilty so easily.

"Come it's time we talked about you coming back home."

I rolled my eyes as I followed him. I looked over my shoulder and found Jeff still staring at me intently.

Chapter Four

I was sitting on the patio having a few beers and some lunch with one of my best friends. The weather was fantastic and I was looking forward to having some girl talk.

I had made a fool of myself at the wedding and I had gotten into another fight with my father about moving back home. I had no intention of doing so and he was steaming mad about it.

"Thanks for letting me crash at your place right now Donna. I swear I will be getting a job soon and will be out of your hair."

"Girl, don't you worry about a thing. I like having the company. Besides I think your dad is kind of nuts."

I laughed. "Yeah…I do have an interview tomorrow at a company in town. They are looking for a secretary and I think I'm a shoe in for the job."

"That's great Carrie. I hope you get it."

"After that it won't be long before I can give you some cash for rent, I promise."

"No problem girl. Don't worry about it. I'm happy to help. So what are you going to do about the mystery dude?"

I had told Donna all about the incident at the wedding with Jeff and she had found it rather amusing to say the least.

"No, I don't expect to ever hear from him again. It's not like we exchanged numbers so there is nothing really for me to do."

"You have to track him down; he sounded amazing."

"Are you serious? I almost hooked up in the bathroom with a complete stranger. It's best I just leave that one alone."

"But you guys had insane chemistry. Don't you know how hard that is to find?"

"Don't start."

"So you're really not gonna see this guy again?"

"Even if I was curious about him, which I'm not, how would I even find him? I have no idea how he knew the couple at the wedding. He could have been a wedding crasher for all I know."

"Hmmm. That sucks. Maybe you should ask the couple if they know him."

"No, I think I will let things go. It's not meant to be."

"He sounds insanely hot though Carrie. Not to mention the weird connection you have to him. I wouldn't let someone go like that so easily if I were you. For all you know he could be the only guy that makes you feel alive inside."

"Hey! You are taking this way too far. I'm not in love with this guy. Yeah he made me feel differently, but so what? He was also an arrogant turd most of the time."

"Trust me you should try to find him."

"I haven't heard a word from him and why would I? He's probably found someone else to feel up by now."

Donna laughed. "Well good luck with the job anyways, at least that one you have in the bag." She winked.

Chapter Five

Jeff

Showering quickly as I was running late for the office. I had a client meeting first thing in the morning as well as an interview and I was already running late. I dressed in a dark blue suit and put a tie around my neck. I never worried much about power ties; if a man really needed one he didn't have that much power.

I grabbed a cup of coffee on my way out the door and made a bee-line for my Camaro. I run a division in my father's company, and I thrived on the work. Well…he technically wasn't my father. He had adopted me as a baby, but he was the only father that I knew and he took really good care of me.

I pulled the Camaro into the parking lot and found my spot, putting the car into park. As I made my way up to the floor my office resided on, I nodded at a few people. My right hand man, Curtis was waiting for me when I got off the elevator.

"What do you have for me Curtis?"

"The temp agency is sending over a girl today to interview for the secretary position."

"Fantastic. See her in when she arrives."

Curtis went about his duties as I got settled into my office chair.

When Carrie walked into my office that afternoon, I was shocked to see her. "Carrie, what are you doing here?"

Curtis looked stunned that I knew her and Carrie just stood there with her mouth hung open.

"Jeff, you know her?"

"Well sort of. What is she doing her?"

Curtis looked a little concerned that he had somehow made a mistake. "Jeff, she is interviewing for the secretary position…is everything okay."

Okay Jeff, get a grip on yourself.

"Yes, of course. I'll handle it from here."

From the moment I met Carrie she had been all I had thought about. I had not forgotten how beautiful she was but seeing her in my office reminded me all over again what a smoke show she was. The girl was hot to say the least. She looked like she had walked right out of a magazine. Could I really hire someone that I was so attracted to? How would I get any work done? She would have my cock hard all day long.

Curtis left the office and Carrie proceeded to glare at me from across the room.

"Please have a seat Carrie; it's nice to see you again."

"Yeah, I bet. Are you seriously going to interview me because I really need this job and I feel like you are going to screw this up for me?"

"I'm not trying to screw anything up for you Carrie. I had no idea that you were interviewing for the position."

"So, what you would be my boss?"

"Yes, essentially though you would be the secretary for the whole division. Does that make you uncomfortable?"

"I don't know."

"I can understand why you might feel a little uneasy after what happened between us at the wedding but I assure you that I will be completely professional in the office. Aside from that I think that you would be great for the job and it's yours if you want it."

"That's it? You are just going to give me the job?"

"Well you said you really needed it, didn't you?"

"I'm not going to lie to you. I wish you weren't going to be my boss. But I need this job too badly so that I don't have to move back in with my dad."

"You want the job? You got it. But don't tell me you have any regrets after."

She chuckled. "I'm sure I will survive."

Chapter Six

To say that I loved my new job was the understatement of the year. I got to work with a great crew of people and the pay was amazing. I would be able to save up for my own apartment soon enough. In the meantime I paid Donna rent and we had a blast living together. The exciting part was that I got to travel with Jeff whenever he had to go away on business trips. It wasn't all about answering the phone to getting coffee; it was always something different every day. The job seemed so much more high profile than I had thought and that made going to work feel like fun instead of a chore. The next week for us was a crazy time as Jeff had taken me to France for a business meeting. It was something I had ever only dreamed about and yet off we flew like it was nothing. I knew Jeff was a successful person, but he was so young to be in his position.

Jeff was still his arrogant self at times but I just chose to ignore it. The one thing that got under my skin more than anything was the fact that his eyes often lingered on me for too long. The problem with me was that I liked the way he looked at me. He just made me feel like I had no control over my feelings. In Paris however I had my own room so I didn't have to worry yet about any type of sexual harassment.

Jeff

I had bonuses to give out to my employees for exception work and Carrie was going to get hers personally. I didn't know how I would have survived the past two weeks without her; she really was a hard worker. I was writing notes for my meeting in my hotel suite when Carrie walked in. She was wearing a tight white sweater that draped off her shoulder and matching linen pants that hugged that ass I loved so much. I could barely think straight when I saw her. I didn't see any pantie lines so there was a good chance that Carrie wasn't wearing any. My God she was so hot. I wondered if she had ever been bent over a piece of furniture before.

"Wow Carrie, you look great." She looked more than great. She made my cock rock hard. One minute I thought of her as an exceptional employee and the next thing I knew I wanted to ravage her.

"Thank you," she blushed deeply. I wondered if she ever thought of fucking me also. I couldn't help but wonder what it would be like to hear her moan my name.

Something new had been happening between us lately. At the very least we had developed a friendship out of the whole thing. I no longer felt awkward working with her and she actually made me want to come into work more often.

She was a little younger than me however and definitely an employee. I should probably keep that in mind every time I thought about bending her over my office desk.

"I have something for you Carrie."

"What's that?" She suddenly looked suspicious of me.

I couldn't blame her, I was literally thinking about what it would be like to be inside of her. Those pants she was wearing were going to be the death of me.

"Around this time of year I give out bonuses to every one of my employees who have been exceptional. I feel like you have earned one as well, you have truly been a life saver these past few weeks."

"Are you sure? I've only been here for a short time." She looked shocked at the idea that she would get a bonus too.

"Yes, I'm completely sure."

She grinned from ear to ear and the look on her face put a smile on mine. I handed her the envelope and watched as she opened it. Her mouth dropped open and she looked up at me. "It's too much."

"No, it's not. Everyone gets the same it's not like I'm playing favorites."

"Well thank you Jeff. This is great."

Just watching her enjoy the moment made me hard all over again. "Maybe you can buy yourself something nice in Paris to bring home with you."

"Oh god, that would be so great." Looking at her I realized in that moment that I was starting to care about Carrie, more than I thought I would.

Chapter Seven

I was still on cloud nine from my trip to Paris with Jeff. He had taken me shopping for couture after all our work was completed. Everything was so high fashion I couldn't believe that I was going to wear some of it. I had used some of my bonus for clothing but I also put a lot of it in savings to insure that I would never have to move back home with my dad. Those days were behind me now and I was determined to live a little. To say that I was lucky would be the understatement of the year. It was amazing to have seen Paris; it was something that I thought I would never be able to do.

Things had been really different between Jeff and I but in a good way. I hadn't expected to like him so much. He wasn't as bad as I originally had thought. Yes he still had his arrogant moments but there was a lot more to Jeff than I had believed. I was just beginning to peel the layers away from who he really was. The thing I liked most about Jeff was that he was very over protective of me. You would think I would hate that after living with my dad and being one of the flock. But he wasn't like that at all.

I sat talking to Donna about my whole trip and it was good to be back at home where I was supposed to be. My life was really starting to look up and it was all thanks to Jeff.

"So how was the fancy vacation? I was stuck at home being jealous in case you were wondering."

I laughed. "It was hardly a vacation, it was mostly work. But when it was all done we spent a day sightseeing and we went shopping. It was pretty great. I got some new clothes."

"Yes, I noticed the bags. I'm really happy for you Carrie. It looks like things are starting to turn around for you."

"Tell me about it. When I returned home I had about a dozen messages on my phone from my dad. Why can't he just let me figure things out on my own?"

"Because you're 18."

"So are you!" I said laughing.

"I know and believe me my parents grill me as well. Not as bad as your dad however, but they still don't think I should be living on my own."

"So the money…was that the only bonus he gave you?"

"Donna!"

"Well do I need to remind you about the bathroom scene?"

"No. I don't need to be reminded of it. I plead temporary insanity."

"I'm sure you do. But anyways I'm just kidding. You must have had a blast in Paris, I can't even imagine."

"Yes, even when working Paris is so glamourous. I can't believe people live there year round."

"Oh I can imagine…or maybe I can't." She said laughing. "So how are things with you and Jeff?"

"Better, I mean I saw him in a whole other light while we were away. And before you give me some smartass remark, it wasn't naked."

"So are you thinking of getting together with him? I thought you didn't want to go there?"

"Well, I don't know. Maybe. Things have just changed a little since I have been working with him. He seems sort of great." I laughed. "Maybe, I'm crazy, I don't know."

"Well, what are you going to do about it?"

"I'm not sure. Should I really be doing anything? Seriously, he's now my boss. I don't want to lose such a great job over whatever is going on between us. What if we break up?"

"I don't know Carrie. That's a tough one. If you think you guys are good for each other I wouldn't just let that go."

"Yeah, maybe."

"Hey, you only live once and that guy is hot."

I laughed, "You are a real big help you know."

Donna was right; it was a hard decision and one that I would have to make on my own. I just feared I would be making a huge mistake.

Jeff

Working late at the office seemed to be a regular thing for me. No matter what, I never seemed to be able to get home early. I thrived on work and being a success within the company was a big deal for me. The office was bustling forward in motion since we returned from France. The meetings had been a success and we had brought in more business. Carrie had the day off since she had spent a whole week in France working. I had a hard time leaving the company because I liked to drip my hands into every project. I was on the forefront of the big deals and I expected to have another promotion by the end of the year.

My right hand man Curtis was always on top of things so I was rarely caught off guard by anything. He rarely made mistakes and he made sure that my job was easy.

When my stomach started grumbling I considered taking a break from work to get some food. I could have Curtis order something in, but maybe a walk would clear my head a little better anyways. In fact maybe I could just leave the rest until morning and go have a late dinner and a few drinks. I started shutting things down and put on my jacket when I heard her.

"Hi Jeff."

I looked up to find Carrie in my office wearing a tight red dress. I had never seen her like that even in Paris. She looked fantastic.

Her hair was down, curled and tussled around her shoulders. She was the most breathtaking thing I had seen in some time. She had taken gorgeous to a whole new level.

"You look stunning. What are you doing here?"

She smiled from ear to ear and that just made her even more beautiful. I had originally thought she was a little sweet and innocent but in that dress there was just no way.

"Thank you. You don't look so bad yourself."

There was something different about Carrie; I couldn't quite figure it out. Was she drunk? She just seemed to walk into my office and ooze seduction. For the most part it had appeared as if she was avoiding me since the bathroom scene.

"What brings you here? Not that I'm going to complain but you know you had the day off."

Things had definitely changed between Carrie and I lately. We had grown closer since we started working together and I no longer felt like she despised me. While in France there had been a few nights where we had stayed up late talking but it had never led to anything so I got comfortable with the idea that nothing was ever going to happen between us. That idea was shot out of the park as soon as she walked in my office in that dress. All I could think about was getting her out of it.

"I wanted to see you. Is that so wrong?"

"No, of course not. I'm just surprised."

She wanted to see me. What did that mean? Was she now coming on to me, because that seemed too good to be true?

I considered approaching her and seeing if she would let me lift her dress a little bit. There was a good chance that I would be slapped. Looking at her right then it seemed it could go either way for me.

Fuck it. I walked up to her as if I could not control myself. She made me feel like a kid in a candy store.

"You have never mentioned of you had a boyfriend Carrie."

She looked down at her feet and my eyes followed as well. She was wearing silver strappy heels that went well with her dress.

"I've never talked to you about things like that because I thought it would be unprofessional in the workplace.

"So is that a yes?"

"No, it's not. I just wasn't sure about us at first."

"Look, I was just about to go out for something to eat would you like to join me? We can talk about whatever you want."

She looked into my eyes and I swear I could get lost in them. *God, she's gorgeous.*

"I'm not sure that's the best idea Jeff. Besides I sort of came here for something else."

"What's that?"

She was still looking at me that way. I couldn't read her at all. I brushed the hair out of her eyes and stepped real close to her. My heart was beating wildly and I hoped that I was making the right decision. I wasn't in the mood to get slapped. I had to go for it though. I need her badly.

"I have wanted you since the moment I met you Carrie, I'm sure you realized that. When I saw you at the wedding I thought you were the most beautiful woman I had ever seen."

"Oh stop."

"No, I'm serious."

"Well I may have had my reservations at first but I don't feel that way any longer."

That was all I needed to hear. I was going to finally kiss this woman and claim her as my own. I was going to make her pretty little mouth swollen from my kisses.

When she locked her eyes to mine it just caused my whole body to heat up. I pulled her to me and kissed her hard. Tasting her mouth caused me to grow rock hard. I needed to be inside of her as soon as possible. My hands found her breasts and I massaged them through her dress. She moaned softly against my lips. My hands went around her and I fumbled at the zipper on her dress.

"Jeff, wait, what if someone walks in?"

"Carrie, I don't care. I need you so badly, if I don't have you I will lose it."

She looked unsure and I kissed her mouth softly to get her back into the flow of things. I doubted there were many other people in the office at that hour and even fewer that would need to disturb me. I went back to work on her dress.

"Jeff, I'm scared."

I looked down at her and her sweet doe eyes as they looked up at me. I cared for her there was no doubt about it. But looking at her just made my cock grow harder.

"There is nothing to be scared of Carrie. I'm going to make you feel so good."

I decided to stop fumbling with her dress. I wanted her right then and there and the more we talked about it the less I felt good about things. I picked her up and carried her to my desk. I didn't care what was on my desk in that moment it was all far less important than Carrie. I had every intention of fucking my secretary on my desk. I pushed up her dress and she gasped. I put my hand between her legs and realized she had no panties on.

"You're a naughty girl Carrie."

She smiled mischievously. I knew then that she had planned on fucking me when she arrived at my office. The very thought of it almost drove me insane. I started rubbing her clit as she grew wet against my fingers.

"Jeff wait."

I looked up at her and she was pointing to something. I turned and saw that she was referring to the fact that one side of my office was all windows and there were no blinds. It hadn't occurred to me that people could see us. I knew there was no way in hell she would let me fuck her for the entire city to see. I went and turn the lights off so that we were immersed in the dark.

"Is that better? No one can see us now."

"Okay." She whispered.

I would not be able to see her body as well but there would be other times I was sure of it. I returned to her and started rubbing her clit once again. I went about in a circular pattern as she moaned against me.

"Oh Jeff."

"Oh baby, I am going to make you feel incredible."

I slid a finger into her pussy and listening to the soft moan. She was so ready for me. I finger fucked her pussy loving how wet she got against my finger. I planned on giving her so much pleasure.

"I need you Jeff."

I began undoing my pants. They dropped to my ankles as I stepped out of them. Carrie lies back on the desk and spread her legs wide for me. It was the sexiest thing I had ever seen. Her mouth already looked swollen from my kisses as I bent forward to claim her mouth once again. I wished that I had taken the time to get her out of that dress, but this would not be the first time I would be fucking her. I planned on tasting every inch of that body.

When I slid inside her she whispered against my shoulder, "I knew your cock would be big."

I loved the sound of her voice saying naughty things to me. I pushed in all the way and listened to her moan. Her pussy was so wet and warm around my cock. I began to rock inside of her until I filled her up completely. She moaned loudly and it caused me to push inside her harder. I kissed her face as I talked to her, riding inside her slowly. I started to pump inside her a little faster until she was crying out my name in ecstasy. I had to admit that it was the best sound in the world. Just being inside her made me horny all over again. I started pounding inside her harder; her warm pussy was causing me to lose all sense of reason. Her orgasm exploded around my cock as I rode her hard and I spilled inside her shortly after.

I could barely catch my breath and I was so close to her that I could smell her sweet perfume. I looked at her and smiled. I could barely see her in the dark but I could tell she was smiling back at me. I kissed her deeply on the lips.

"How are you doing Carrie?"

I slowly exited her pussy and began to clean myself. "It looks like I had my dessert first. Want to go have that dinner?"

"Sure let's do that."

I was tempted to go at it a second time but there would always be another time.

Carrie sat up and started to straighten out her dress. She still looked incredible, probably better than when she walked in. When she stood up I gave her a little tap on her ass.

"We should probably go. I'm definitely starving now." She said with a giggle.

I nodded and I kissed her one last time before we headed out the door.

Chapter Eight

Carrie

We had a hard time controlling ourselves at the office. Every time we were near each other we couldn't keep our hands off one another. I would go in and give him some reports or an article to look over and the next thing I knew we were going at it. We always turned the lights off so that if anyone was in the office they wouldn't come looking for Jeff, that and those damn windows. It was pretty fun though I had to admit going in and getting a quickie from Jeff or even have him lick my pussy for 15 minutes. I couldn't get enough of him. We had been having so much sex in the dark that I was starting to wonder what the guy actually looked like in the buff. Not that I worried though, Jeff was hot as hell.

There we stood once again in his office trying to maintain some self-control and it wasn't easy. I wondered if people in the office were starting to suspect our indiscretions. I was such a cliché in that moment. It sure wasn't the first time a secretary got caught sleeping with her boss. That was why I was so worried about people finding out at first. I needed to see where things were going with Jeff and I first. If it was just going to be a fling then there was no reason for anyone to know. I didn't want people to think that I was some kind of tramp. If things progressed between Jeff and I then I would be okay with people at the office finding out. But things were too fresh and new…and sexual for me to be okay with people finding out.

"So how is your day going sweetheart?"

"Oh, it's wonderful thank you."

"Have I told you how lovely you look today?"

"Yes, you tell me every day and then you try to get in my pants."

"Oh, now that sounds like a good idea. There is just something about your mouth that makes my cock hard."

He pulled me to him and kissed me hard. My heart was beating furiously in my chest; it felt like it was going to break free. There was just something about being that close to Jeff that just felt right. I felt so connected to him in so many ways. The moment he touched me he made me so incredibly horny. His tongue continued to play with mine and I pulled him over to his desk.

Jeff just stared at me. He wanted me just as badly as I wanted him. It was written all over his face.

"I want your pussy again Carrie."

 I smiled up at him, his words turning me on more.

Jeff leaned in and slipped his hand around my neck pulling me into him as his mouth claimed mine. I could taste the coffee he had been drinking at his desk.

"Let me sit down baby. I want you to sit on my cock and ride it."

He undid his pants and let them fall to the floor; He sat down in his office chair and watched as I lifted up my skirt. I knew I was already wet and ready to take his cock. I grinned loving the sound of his words. I got into position with my back facing him and plunged myself onto his cock. Jeff was pushed right up against my g-spot in that position and the feeling made me just about lose my mind.

I was rendered speechless and I started moving slowly. He felt fantastic and I started riding his smooth cock even harder. He was moaning softly as well and it was making me lose control.

"Mmmm, Carrie you sexy girl. You feel delicious. You ride my cock good baby."

I moaned, his voice, his words his cock was driving me mad. And just when I thought it couldn't get any better he reached around and started playing with my clit. It was almost too much to bear, I couldn't get enough. I was moaning softly wanting to beg for more but feeling already possessed by him. My pussy was so wet, he was driving me wild.

"Just relax sweetheart." I gasped as pleasure coursed through to me. I continued pumping onto his cock as an orgasm took a hold of me once again. "Oh god Jeff, oh god that feels so god," I whispered my yearnings to him.

"I want to put my cock in you and fuck you. It's my turn."

I lifted myself off his cock and waited to see what he had in mind.

His cock, oh god, looking at his size made me horny all over again. I wanted to be fucked by him desperately. He was all I could think about throughout the day. I need him and wanted him daily. Was that so wrong?

I couldn't believe all that was happening, it was hard to believe I was in that situation, right there in his office again but I loved every moment of it. Jeff caused my body to throb immensely until I wanted to beg him to release me from that feeling. I needed him at that point, to fuck me nice and hard.

He got up from the desk and pushed me against it. I lay out on my desk and when he pushed my legs up over my head my eyes widened. It was a good thing I was flexible.

I did as I was told, my body weakened from pleasure. I was lying on my back, my legs spread before him and above him.

He positioned himself in the missionary position and put my legs up over my head. He entered me slowly and I gasped with how deep he went.

"Oh yes, this is nice. You're nice and tight baby. God your pussy feels so good." The level of deepness in that position was crazy good.

I leaned my head back, delirious with pleasure. Jeff fit inside me perfectly and I got a wave of pleasure every time he moved inside me. He began pumping me a little faster, causing me to moan loudly. His cock was perfect and with the position we were using he was in the perfect spot to hit my G-spot over and over again. My body built up once again and I knew that he was going to cause me to cum all over his cock.

"Cum for me baby, I can see it on your face. Cum on my cock, I want it baby."

I exploded then doing as he asked, moaning his name. I was spent and yet he kept fucking me slowly. He pulled out and pulled me off the desk. I followed him around his desk and he told me to lie down on the floor. I quickly looked at the door and was amazed that we had not been discovered at that point. We had fucked in his office a few times now and hopefully no one was the wiser.

"I can't get enough of your ass in my hands Carrie."

Jeff slid inside my pussy hard. I cried out as pleasure over took my body. I was on my back but he positioned me so that his hands grasped under my ass and he lifted me up and supported my weight. The only think on the ground were my shoulders and I wrapped my legs around his waist. I moaned, enjoying every inch of his cock as he pounded me over and over again. He leaned down towards me and spanked my ass. I cried out realizing I had never experienced anything so sexy in my entire life. He pumped into me harder waves of pleasure rolling off of me. I smiled up at him and stifled my moans as best I could as another orgasm ripped through me. I was having multiple orgasms with this man, how was I ever to return to normal sex again?

"You have a real nice pussy Carrie, I like fucking you."

I moaned loving the way Jeff was making me feel, but even more so by the way he talked to me.

He pulled out again and laid me down gently on the floor. He slid his fingers into my pussy and finger fucked me for a bit, he was making me wet all over again, although at that point I was pretty soaked from all the fucking. "I want you back on my cock baby, will you sit on me again and ride me good."

"You bet your ass I will."

He returned to the desk and sat himself of the edge of it. I positioned myself so I had my back to him again and slid his cock inside me.

"There we go darling; we are going to go easy. That feels good doesn't it?" I moaned in agreement.

"Okay, here we go, just stay relaxed, don't tense up."

I could hardly believe myself at that moment what had ever possessed me to do such a thing, having sex with my boss in his office? What would Curtis think? God, I had wanted Jeff so badly, I still did. I was so sexually satisfied but yet so horny still I would have let him do just about anything to me. I was aching inside with want of him. I had never thought of having sex in his office before, it just never occurred to me to try such a thing. I hadn't realized the pleasure that could be brought to me by such a destination.

I rode Jeff's cock feeling the delicious sensations spread all over my body.

"Just relax sweetheart, you are tensing up. I can feel you hugging my cock."

I hadn't realized that I was holding my breath so I did as he said. As I pushed onto him a little more I tried to relax and allowed it to happen. He certainly felt huge when he was going in on this end. I felt full with him in my pussy. He then began to move his hips and meet my thrusts onto his cock. I moaned as he picked up the pace, his smooth cock gliding inside and out.

"How does it feel Carrie?"

"So good," I whispered.

"That's what I like to hear baby."

"I love learning new positions with you."

The thought of having a variety of positions available to me had never occurred to me but it sounded like a hot idea and it was one of the things that I like most about our sex life. Riding on him he felt humongous inside me. He rocked into me slowly continuing to meet my thrusts. I started rocking into him faster letting the waves of pleasure crash into me repeatedly, not much break in between.

"Oh god," I moaned.

He reached around and felt for my pussy. He rubbed against my moist clit giving me some added pleasure while he moved his cock inside me.

"Okay baby, I want you to fuck me good."

I thought I would lose my mind with the words coming out of his mouth. The whole length of his cock slowly pushed inside me causing me to let out a slow and powerful moan. There were so many different feelings and sensations going through my body at that moment. I was lost in a sea of pleasure and I wanted to let go of another orgasm.

"Oh God Jeff, your cock feels so good."

He started pumping me as I thrust onto him. I was delirious with the pleasure he was giving me, I needed it, needed him.

My pussy was soaked. I was dripping wet and I felt a buildup once again. I couldn't believe I was about to cum again. God, the thought was just too delicious.

"Jeff, it feels good, it really does feel so good."

"I know baby. It's amazing isn't it?"

"Yes," I gasped, "I'm coming again."

My whole body shuddered as I came. He continued pumping inside of me breaking all reason inside my mind. He was so sexy; all of it was so incredible. As I felt myself build up for another orgasm, the shudders ripped through my body causing me to ache to scream his name.

"Oh Carrie, I'm ready too baby. I'm going to fill up your pussy with a load."

I moaned loving how sexy he was with his dirty talk. He spilled inside of me and collapsed against his desk.

I slid slowly off of his cock and smiled as I cleaned myself off. I composed myself and straightened out my skirt.

I bent down and kissed him hard on the mouth.

"Until next time Jeff." I winked as I walked out the door leaving him there panting.

Jeff

The past few days with Carrie had been some of the best that I could remember when it came to dating girls. She was really something special. We had been spending a lot of time together while I wined and dined her. We hadn't had sex again since the first time but I was a patient man. I could barely concentrate at work when it came to Carrie; I was beginning to think that I was addicted to the girl. The more I got to know her the more I realized that there wasn't a thing that I didn't like about her.

At the office we kept things low-key, neither of us was ready to have coworkers know that there was something between us. I would do anything for Carrie, however, so if there was a chance she wasn't comfortable with the secret I would tell everyone. Carrie was deeper than I had originally thought. She loved foreign films and she could read a book in a day. She had quite the sheltered life when she had been living with her dad, so it was easy for her to want to seek out adventure as much as possible. She could be a little wild child when she wanted to be.

Carrie walked into my apartment then with a smile on her face. "You really worked late tonight. How come? The office was looking pretty empty when I left. You don't have to work all night you know."

I smiled at her. Carrie was wearing a cashmere sweater that she had purchased while we were in France. She was a vision.

"Yes, I know. How are you today? You look fantastic."

"Thank you. Where are we going with this Jeff?"

"Wherever you want it to go."

She smiled softly and I had to wonder what was going on in her head. What did she want?

"How about some dinner? Maybe we can talk about it all."

"Sure."

"You really do look beautiful Carrie. You should shop in Paris more often."

"Yeah I wish." Her cheeks burned red. She was cute as a button when she blushed. I got up from my desk and pulled her towards me. Kissing her she moaned underneath my lips. She lit me up immediately; the chemistry between us just ignited the moment. There was just something about kissing her that got me instantly hard.

I kissed her and my hands found their way to her face. My tongue found hers at the same time that my hands left her face to squeeze her ass. She really had a nice ass and I loved a squeezing it in my hands.

"I want you Jeff, right now."

"That's the best thing I've heard all day."

Carrie

Jeff just stared at me, I could tell he was feeling exactly the same way that I was. He wanted me and I remembered what it had been like for him to be inside of me.

"I want you so much Jeff."

He flashed me a devilish grin that made me warm all over. "I'm going to make you feel really good Carrie by doing dirty things to you. This time we are keeping the lights on."

I gasped; no one had ever talked that way to me before. Yes I wouldn't mind having the lights on as well. I wanted to see him naked as well.

He leaned in and slipped his hand around my neck pulling me in to him as his mouth claimed mine. He tasted sweet and alluring. His mouth was hot to the touch and I almost moaned at his touch. He kissed me softly at first and then his kisses became more fevered as if he needed my mouth on his. His tongue slipped into my mouth and I claimed it. I sucked him slowly, tasting him before I pulled away. He pulled me in again as he was not finished kissing me. His tongue found mine again and our kisses grew more passionate. His hand found my breast and he kneaded it softly. He began pulling off my sweater. He stopped kissing me momentarily to look down at my breasts that were dying to be released from my bra.

"You are beautiful."

He pulled me over to the couch. I smiled though all I could think about was what he looked like naked. Jeff unclasped my bra and he pushed me back down on the couch. His mouth found my nipple and he sucked, nipped and licked it. The sensation I was getting was making my panties wet. I moaned softly as he replaced his mouth with his fingers and pulled on my nipple causing a slight pain. I liked it, it made me horny. Jeff continued playing with my nipples causing me to moan as a pleasure built up in my body. My hand reached down and I massaged the front of his pants, I could feel his hard cock pushing against his pants. He smiled down at me. "Do you want it? Do you want it in your mouth?"

I nodded, still speechless by the things that came out of his mouth. I felt wanton around him, like I would do just about anything for pleasure. To have him please my body, to give me what I wanted. He undid his button and pulled the zipper on his pants down. He brought his pants down to his knees and slid his underwear down with them. His hard cock bounced before me now free from his underwear. He came above me and I took his cock into my mouth and sucked on it. His eyes closed above me and I sucked hard while I massaged his balls. My tongue began to swirl against his shaft and then around his tip. Jeff moaned with eagerness and I sucked him even harder.

"Oh god, you're good at this."

I took his cock deeper into my mouth until it hit the back of my throat. I moved up and down rhythmically until I moved fluidly with him in my mouth.

His moans excited me and I felt my pussy become wetter. He pulled his cock out of my mouth and finished undressing himself. I followed suit and undid my dress pants and slipped them off. I was only wearing a thong underneath so it was easy to dispose of. He watched me undress and he couldn't take his eyes off my pussy.

"Mmm, you look good. Maybe good enough to eat Carrie."

I had not done very much oral with anyone so the idea of him between my legs made me nervous. I didn't hesitate however to lean back down on the seat and spread my legs. I had just shaved the other day so I was nice and fresh for him.

He bent forward and licked my pussy slowly as if he was licking an ice cream cone on a hot summer day. It felt incredible as his tongue licked the sides of my opening, causing a tingle to run through my body. He took my clit in his mouth and sucked on it causing me to moan loudly as my pussy dripped.

"Oh god...oh god..."

Jeff looked up and smiled, "Does that feel good sweetheart?"

"Oh god yes it feels incredible."

My pussy was dripping and he was licking it up tasting every inch of me. I felt the buildup coming. I was going to cum right there on his couch.

"Oh God, oh wow, I'm going to cum."

Jeff was sucking on my clit when he buried a finger inside my pussy and started pumping away. It was too much, too much all at once and I cried out as I had an orgasm so delicious that I wanted even more.

"How was that?"

I just grinned with desire written all over my face.

"Now turn over." I did so readily not really understanding why.

"I want to lick your hot little ass."

Confused I asked, "My what?"

"Your hot little ass, I'm going to lick you nice."

I was rendered speechless and I wasn't sure if I should object or not. Was he really going to put his tongue there? Was that okay?

I was bent over on the couch in the doggy style position with my ass in the air. I felt him shift positions and then I felt it. He spread

48

my cheeks, bent over and licked my ass. I gasped at the sensation it brought as I had never anticipated that it would feel that way. It was very similar to having the lips of your pussy licked and I closed my eyes as desire built up.

"Mmmm, you dirty girl. You taste delicious."

I moaned, his voice, his words his tongue was driving me mad. And just when I thought it couldn't get any better he buried a finger inside my pussy and finger fucked me while he licked my ass. It was almost too much to bear, I couldn't get enough. I was moaning loudly wanting to beg for more but feeling so shy. My pussy was so wet, he was driving me wild. He took his fingers out wet with me all over them and started rubbing them against my ass.

I tensed up unsure of what he was about to do to me next.

"Just relax sweetheart." He slowly inserted his finger into my ass. I gasped as a combination of pleasure and pain coursed through to me. I wasn't sure if I liked it until he continued to push his finger inside me. There was more pleasure and just a bit of pain. He started fingering my ass and I couldn't understand the different waves of pleasure that ripped through me.

"How are you doing? Everything okay Carrie?"

"Yes, I've never done this before."

"I can tell. You have a tight little ass. I want to put my cock inside it and fuck you proper."

His cock, oh God, I wasn't sure it could fit inside me. His finger caused some pain what would his cock feel like? I had never done anything like that before.

"I don't know."

"I'm fucking your ass Carrie. You will like it, trust me."

I closed my eyes; his forcefulness turned me on so I would allow him to take what he wanted. I couldn't believe all that was happening it was hard to believe I was in that situation but I loved every moment of it. He caused my body to throb immensely until I wanted to beg him to release me from that feeling. I needed him at that point, to fuck me good as he said it so that I would get the release that I wanted, the release that I deserved.

"Turn over sweetheart."

I did as I was told, my body weakened from pleasure. I was lying on my back, my legs spread before him.

"Touch yourself for me."

My eyes popped open. I shook my head, "I can't."

"Yes, you can. I want to see you please yourself it turns me on and then I'm going to slide inside that wet pussy of yours and fuck you really good."

Nervousness swelled inside my stomach, I had masturbated before obviously, but never in front of anyone. Compared to Jeff my sex life had been pretty vanilla before. I thought I was living with some pretty steamy sex stories but it turned out that I was missing out on a lot of pleasure. So I did what any sane woman would do and I spread my legs and slid my fingers through the wetness that was all over my pussy. I swirled it around before moving up to my clit, massaging it with my finger. I grinded into it closing my eyes as I enjoyed my own touch. I was sure my face was a bright crimson but Jeff didn't say a thing. In fact when I opened my eyes he was staring down at me mesmerized by what I was doing. He looked up at me with fire in his eyes and the look on his face made me feel incredible. Like I was completely in control of his pleasure. I loved the feeling of controlling his lust and I inserted two fingers inside my pussy and moaned as they went in deep. I finger fucked myself in front of him watching a slow smile form on his face.

"That is so hot."

I moaned as I pleasured myself, taking my fingers out and swirling my juices around my clit. I was throbbing all over and I desperately wanted to be fucked at that point.

"Please?"

"Please what darling, do you want some help?"

50

"I want you."

"Then you can have me." He positioned himself in the missionary position and put my legs up onto his shoulders. Jeff entered me slowly and I gasped with how deep he went.

"Oh yes, this is nice. You're nice and tight baby. God your pussy feels so good."

I leaned my head back, delirious with pleasure. He fit inside me perfectly and I got a wave of pleasure every time he moved inside me. He began pumping me a little faster, causing me to moan loudly. His cock was perfect and with the position we were using he was in the perfect spot to hit my G-spot over and over again. My body built up once again and I knew that he was going to cause me to cum all over his cock.

"Cum for me baby, I can see it on your face. Cum all over my cock."

I exploded then doing as he asked, screaming loudly. I was spent and yet he kept fucking me slowly. He pulled out and then rolled me over. I stuck my ass in the air eager for more cock. I wanted to be fucked well and Jeff was certainly the man to do it.

"You have such a nice ass; you should see this glorious view that I have."

He slid inside my pussy hard. I cried out as pleasure over took my body. Doggy style was meant for a little rougher action and he was showing me just that. I moaned, enjoying every inch of his cock as he pounded me over and over again. He leaned down towards me and bit my shoulder. I cried out realizing I had never experienced anything so sexy in my entire life. He pumped into me harder waves of pleasure rolling off of me. My moans were becoming screams as an orgasm ripped through me. I was having multiple orgasms with this man, how was I ever to return to normal sex again?

"You have a real nice pussy Carrie, I like fucking you. I wish I could pump you full of cum but I really want to feel what your ass feels like."

I moaned, loving the way he was making me feel, but even more so by the way he talked to me.

"Can I spread your cheeks and fuck your ass baby?"

"Oh god...I don't know Jeff. Is it going to hurt me?"

"It will at first but that will go away. You will feel pleasure as well. I assure you, you will enjoy my cock in your ass. We will go slowly so that I don't hurt you. I will put the tip in and we'll ease him in from there."

"Okay." He slid his fingers into my pussy and finger fucked me for a bit, he was making me wet all over again, although at that point I was pretty soaked from all the fucking. He took his fingers out and rubbed my juices all over his cock, providing a lubricant. He also rubbed my ass with my pussy juices and inserted a finger slowly into my ass causing me to moan.

"There we go darling; we are going to go easy. That feels good doesn't it?" I moaned in agreement.

"Okay, here we go, just stay relaxed, don't tense up."

I was about to have anal sex for the first time in my life with Jeff. I could hardly believe myself at that moment what had ever possessed me to do such a thing? God, I had wanted him so badly, I still did. I was so sexually satisfied but yet so horny still I would have let him do just about anything to me. I was aching inside with want of him. I had never thought of having anal sex before, it just never occurred to me to try such a thing. I hadn't realized the pleasure that could be brought to me by such an act. I always thought guys who wanted it were pigs, but Jeff was no pig; he just wanted to bring as much pleasure to my body as I could stand.

He pushed into my ass and a sharp pain went through me causing me to gasp. "Just relax sweetheart, you are tensing up. Let out the breath you're holding in."

I hadn't realized that I was holding my breath so I did as he said. He began fucking me with just the tip of his cock in my ass. It was true that there were equal measures of pain and pleasure coursing

52

through my body. The pain made me ache for him to stop but the bursts of pleasure that came through made me want to continue to see what his full length felt like. As Jeff pushed inside me a little more I tried to relax and allowed it to happen. He certainly felt huge when he was going in on this end. I felt full with him in my ass, while he was stationary waiting to let my ass get used to the change. He then began to fuck me again, trying to allow me to get used to more inside of me. I moaned as he picked up the pace, his smooth cock gliding inside and out.

"Are you okay Carrie?"

"Yes," I whispered.

"Does it feel good?"

"It's very different, but not in a bad way. If I ignore the pain it feels quite good."

"Well the more you do it the less pain you will experience. You would be able to take my cock easily with practice."

The thought of having regular anal sex had never occurred to me but it sounded like a hot idea. He pushed inside a little bit more and I cried out. I tried to relax; it already felt like he was all the way in even though he was only half way. He felt humongous inside me. He rocked into me slowly letting my body get used to him all over again. When he felt I had, he pumped me faster letting the waves of pleasure crash into me repeatedly, not much break in between.

"You have such a tight hot ass, I knew the moment I saw you that your ass would feel this good."

"Oh God Jeff," I moaned loudly.

He reached around and felt for my pussy. He rubbed against my moist clit giving me some added pleasure while he moved his cock inside me.

"Okay baby, I want you to take all of me. Then I'm going to give your ass a proper fucking."

I thought I would lose my mind with the words coming out of his mouth. He was sexy and experienced and he was showing me a world I had never thought existed. Or one that I at least never imagined I would venture into.

The whole length of his cock slowly pushed inside me causing me to let out a slow and powerful moan. There were so many different feelings and sensations going through my body at that moment. I was lost in a sea of pain and pleasure and I wanted to let go of one but not at the risk of losing the other.

"I want more."

I heard him chuckle and he started pumping me with the whole length of his cock stretching my ass. I was delirious with the pleasure he was giving me, I needed it, needed him even though our experience together was only to be brief.

What I didn't expect was for my pussy to become so wet due to what he was doing to my ass. I was dripping wet and I felt a buildup once again. I couldn't believe I was about to cum from anal sex. God, the thought was just too delicious.

"Jeff, it feels good, it really does feel good."

"After a while the pleasure just takes over the pain doesn't?"

"Yes," I gasped, "I'm coming again."

My whole body shuddered as I came, because his cock was elsewhere I felt cum dripping down my leg. He continued pumping inside of me breaking all reason inside my mind. He was glorious; all of it was so incredible. The best sex of my life was happening right on Jeff's couch. As I felt myself build up for another orgasm, the shudders ripped through my body causing me to scream out once again.

"Oh Carrie, I'm ready too baby. I'm going to fill up your ass with cum."

I moaned loving how sexy he was with his dirty talk. He spilled inside of me and collapsed softly against my back. I could feel his breath on my back and I was just as spent as he was.

54

He slid slowly out of my ass and I knew for certain that I was going to be very sore the next day. It would have all been worth it. He bent down and kissed my ass and then chuckled.

Still smiling from all my orgasm I asked, "What are you laughing at?"

"I just noticed something on your ass. You have a birthmark; it looks like half a heart."

"Yeah, I've had that since I was a baby." I started to sit up and I turned to him. He looked like he was in shock.

"What is it?"

"I don't know, it's just weird. I have the same birthmark in the exact same spot."

I stared at him unsure of what he was saying. I couldn't even comprehend what he was saying. "What are you talking about?"

"I'm serious. We have the same birthmark." He turned his ass towards me and I saw it. He was right. It was the exact same mark in the exact same spot.

"Holy shit."

"I know, that's weird right?"

He dug around his side table and pulled out some Kleenex's and handed them to me. I cleaned myself off as best that I could and slipped into my thong. I slipped into my pants as I watched him rummaging around for his clothes that had fallen to the floor. Finding them he quickly slipped into underwear and jeans, pulling his t-shirt over his head.

I slid into my bra and put my sweater on. My hands shook from the toile the orgasms took on my body, He was watching me dress and when I looked up at him he smiled. I couldn't smile though; I didn't feel like it at all. My heart was beating hard in my chest and I didn't know what to say or really how to say it.

"What? What's wrong?"

"I don't know. I feel like something is wrong."

"What do you mean?"

I sat back down on the couch. I didn't know what the hell to do. But I had to talk to Jeff about something. I could hardly believe it was true myself but I had to find out if it was for real. God, I hoped that it wasn't real.

"Jeff, you mentioned to me that you were adopted before right?"

He looked at me completely dumbfounded. "Yes, but what does that have to do with anything?"

"Do you have any idea who your real parents are?"

He sighed deeply. "Okay Carrie, you have to tell me what's going on because you are starting to freak me out. One minute I'm having some pretty incredible sex and the next thing I know you are getting all weird over the birthmarks. Granted I think it's a little weird myself but so what?"

"Well you aren't going to like it but I know why we have the same birthmart and it's not good news."

"What the hell are you talking about Carrie?"

"This is going to sound really screwed up and just thinking about it makes me want to throw up. When I was younger I walked in on my parents having sex."

He chuckled. He wouldn't be laughing much longer.

"My father was having sex with my mother doggy style. At first I didn't know what they were doing, I was so young. So I walked into the room, they realized I was in and walked me out of course but not before I saw the same mark that we both have on my father's behind. He is the reason why I have the same birthmark. That's why I was wondering if you knew who your father was."

He looked at me stunned and I knew he was having a hard time processing what I had just told him. I couldn't blame him, it messed me up pretty badly too. I didn't even want to think about what I was saying. It had to be a lie, didn't it? I couldn't imagine that it could be true, but there it was right on both our asses.

"Let me get this straight…you are saying that I could be your brother. You can't be serious."

"Oh, I'm very serious. You have the same birthmark as my father Jeff. Oh my god. I can't believe this but we are related. We are brother and sister."

"Holy shit Carrie. This can't be real. None of that makes any sense."

"You were adopted Jeff and you have the same birthmark as both me and my dad. How else do you explain that?"

"No, it can't be true. We have been having sex; there is no way that you are my sister."

"My parents must have had you when they were young, too young for children. They must have given you up and then I came along. We aren't that far apart in age. About five years, that would make sense because my mother wouldn't even have started college when she had you."

"Carrie, please stop talking like we are siblings."

"Jeff. We need to talk to my dad."

"Oh my god, I can't believe this is happening right now."

I kissed him on the cheek. "I will call you later, I need to figure this out and get a hold of my dad. Are you going to be okay?"

"I'm not sure Carrie. I thought I found the girl of my dreams and it turns out she might be my sister. It's all a little hard to take right now."

I nodded, unsure of what to say. Hell what could I say; I was feeling no different than he was. We had been having sex for weeks not knowing that we were probably related. We had no idea because we had spent all the time in his office fucking with the lights off. Sometimes life liked to throw you some cruel jokes every now and again. I didn't want Jeff to be my brother, but I didn't know how else to explain the birthmark. It looked like things were going to be very different between us whether we like it or not.

"I will call you later. I'm sorry."

He put his head in his hands and I walked out the door. I needed to talk to Donna before I even thought of calling my dad.

Chapter Nine

"Are you serious? No. You can't be serious." I was looking at the shocked look on my best friends face and it actually hurt my heart. I had left Jeff and immediately returned to my apartment in the hopes that Donna was there. When I saw her I immediately burst into tears. She had run over to me and hugged me why I confessed everything to her. She took it as well as expected.

"Holy fuck. I'm totally serious. I have no idea what to do or how my life became so complicated. What did I do to deserve this Donna? This has to be some kind of karma coming back to haunt me."

"It's horrible news Carrie; I can't even imagine how you must feel. Like really…what are the chances of something like that happening."

"I couldn't tell you. But it's a little too fucked up for me."

"So did you know that your parents had another kid that they gave up for adoption?"

"No. I have no idea. I'm just guessing but there is no other explanation right? I wish there was but all roads seem to lead there."

"Yes, I agree. There is no way he should have the same birthmark unless he's…"

She let it hang there in the air between us. I was glad she didn't finish the sentence, I was sick of hearing those words.

"What am I going to do Donna?" Tears welled up in my eyes.

"Okay firstly you need to calm down. In the big scheme of things it's not the end of the world. It's not like you guys knew about it. You will just have to have a different type of relationship."

"I'm falling for this guy Donna. How can I turn that off and start thinking about him as my brother. My god, the things we have done!"

"Okay, okay too much information."

"What am I going to do?"

"Well, you are going to talk to your parents firstly and find out if they had a kid that they gave up for adoption. At least then you will know for sure. After that…well that's where things get tricky."

"I'm going to need years of therapy to get over this."

"Carrie, you are going to be just fine. Either way. I know this is some terribly shocking news but one way or another you will be okay."

"This is one big epic disaster. My life is never going to be the same. Your words are nice but my life is officially messed up. I'm falling in love with a guy that may be my biological brother never mind we have had sex so many ways possible."

"Carrie, I'm really sorry. It really is horrible news. But you need to talk to your father sooner rather than later."

I felt hysterical, that I could just start laughing. And if I started laughing I just wouldn't stop. I spend the night cackling as I slowly lost my mind. That was how I felt about the situation that I was now in.

Chapter Ten

That morning I had called up Jeff and arranged for him to meet me at my apartment. When he arrived things were insanely awkward between us. He had this look of longing in his face and I knew he wanted to touch me. I wanted the same thing too but I just couldn't do it. I knew if I let him close that I would start bawling and that was the last thing we needed right then. I had made arrangements for us to meet up with my parents at their house. I hadn't been back there since I had moved out. I hadn't seen my father since the wedding and even then my mother wasn't there. Seeing them again under these circumstances was not going to be easy.

"How are you?" I asked him.

"I've been better. How about you?"

"Pretty much the same."

"Carrie, I just can't believe this is true. It doesn't seem real. Are you sure about all this?"

I sighed, "No, I'm not. But I do know that we all have the exact same birthmarks and I don't know how else to explain that. Do you?"

"No. I just can't believe this is happening. I just want to kiss you right now and it's so wrong now for me to do so. But how am I supposed to turn those feelings off now?"

"I don't know. This isn't exactly something that I expected either. It's crazy and it should never have happened to us. But it did and now we have to deal with it."

"What if your dad doesn't want to talk about the past?"

"Well he's going to have to because there is a chance that his past will be looking him straight in the face."

Jeff cringed.

"I'm sorry, I shouldn't have said that."

"No, it's okay. It's not your fault. Let's get this over with and go from there."

We left my apartment and took the 20 minute drive to my parents' house. My mother was a little more laid back then my father was but she would be no more interested in having this conversation then my father would. It was going to be one hell of a night. I wasn't looking forward to it and judging by the frown on Jeff's face he wasn't either.

When we arrived we quickly made our way up to the door and knocked. I felt sick to my stomach as I waited for my father to answer the door. It felt like an eternity past before he came and swung the door open.

"Carrie, it's good to see you. I was surprised to get your call that you wanted to see us. It's been a while."

"I know dad, I'm sorry about everything. I just needed to be on my own. I wished you would be able to understand that. I wasn't trying to hurt you. I've been really busy lately. I have a new job, a really good one and I'm doing well."

"Well that is something good to hear for once."

My dad was still being stubborn over the fact that I had left the flock and moved out on my own at such a young age. He was furious that I had not returned back home with my tail between my legs. I was determined to make it on my own however and nothing was going to deter me from that thought. I would have everything that I wanted. Well, maybe not everything.

I turned to Jeff. "Dad, you remember Jeff, he was with me at the wedding."

My dad gave Jeff a once over and sternly looked at him. "Son, if you are here to tell me you got my daughter pregnant, I'm not going to be happy about it."

"Dad!"

Jeff looked stunned and didn't know how to respond. Things were already not going well. They were about to get far worse.

62

"How Howard, leave the kids alone. What is the matter with you? I doubt that Carrie got us all together to tell us that. It's nice to meet you Jeff."

He just nodded and I felt so sorry for him.

"Yeah, well no, we definitely didn't come here to tell you that so you can rest easy."

"Well come inside, the both of you and have a seat. Your mother has made us some coffee and snacks so please help yourself to them."

"Thanks Mom."

She started hanging out coffee mugs and I was grateful for the moment to collect my thoughts. I wasn't entirely sure how I was going to do things. I was winging it for the most part. I didn't know how to say what I had to say tactfully. It probably would have been easier to tell him that I was pregnant. Yes, much easier.

We all sat down in the living room and settled in. I sipped my coffee and looked up at my mother. She smiled at me warmly clearly unfazed by my visit. I think she understood more why I left home than my father did.

"It's so great to see you Carrie."

"It's great to see you too mom."

"Well we would see her more often if she would have stayed home."

I rolled my eyes. My mother thankfully stepped in. "Oh Howard, drop it please. She is on her own now; you need to let it go. I don't want our daughter afraid to come home and visit. If she needs to come home she knows that there is always an open door here for her."

"Thanks mom."

"Okay Carrie, so why did you ask for us all to get together. You said you had something important to talk to us about. So what is it?"

I looked over at Jeff who smiled at me. It gave me the courage to power through what I had to say.

"Mom...dad. I need to know something about your past. I believe something may have happened with you guys in the past that is now affecting my future."

Both my parents frowned, clearly just as confused as I was.

"What do you mean you need to know something about our past? Like what?"

I took a deep breath. "I need to know if you guys had another child before you had me. A child that you gave up for adoption?"

My mother gasped and my father looked furious. My mother couldn't even respond so I knew things weren't looking well for us.

"How dare you come in here and ask such a personal question of us."

Jeff grasped my hand and squeezed it tight.

"I wouldn't ask if it wasn't important dad. I need to know."

"How did you know?" My mother whispered.

I looked over at her stunned.

"Marie! What are you doing?"

"Harold, she obviously knows. Do you think she came up with this out of the blue? Don't be so ridiculous. Carrie, what is going on here? Do you really think that this is an appropriate time to be having this conversation? The first time we meet your boyfriend?"

"No, and I understand why you find this so upsetting. But he is the reason why I found out about the adoption."

My mother was shaking her head. "I don't understand any of this. How did you know Carrie? We have never discussed it since. We didn't even keep any of the paperwork."

"The birthmark. You know the one that we all share? I found out about the adoption because of that."

"What do you mean?" My mother asked.

"This is really difficult for me to say especially since things are so strained between us already. But Jeff has the same birthmark. I have reason to believe that he is your son."

My parents stared at me like I had lost my mind. I couldn't blame them. I certainly felt like I had lost it. What else could I say? I needed them to figure it out on their own now because all I wanted to do was throw up. I was emotionally rung out by everything that had happened between Jeff and I and now things had gone to a whole other level. I didn't know how to deal with it. I looked to Jeff who had gone completely white. He knew what it all meant. It was starting to look like we were siblings after all and I didn't know how to comfort him. I felt lost myself so how could I possibly make him feel any better about the situation.

"You think Jeff is our child. The one we gave up for adoption?" My mother asked. My dad was just staring at Jeff with a blank look on his face.

"Yes."

"You think your boyfriend is your brother?"

"Yes," I said weakly.

My father came into the conversation with a booming voice. "Have you two been having sex?"

"Oh god," I muttered.

"Howard you are completely out of line."

"I'm out of line? Do you even believe what we are hearing right now? Our daughter came here to tell us that she is having sex with her brother. Does that sound about right to you?"

My mother shook her head in disbelief. Things had just gone from bad to worse and I could only imagine them spiralling out of control.

"It just happened Dad, we had no idea. How could we possibly know? It's not like you told me you had a child."

"So you two have had sex?" My father was determined to find out the truth no matter how much embarrassment he caused the room.

"Yes father we have had sex. That is not what we are here to discuss however so drop it. I'm a grown up now whether you want to believe that or not. I'm not here to discuss my sex life with you."

"You should have stayed here and none of this would have ever happened."

"No dad. It would have. I still would have met Jeff at the same wedding. It was inevitable that this would go down the same road that it has."

"What makes you think that he's our son?" My mother whispered. She looked shell shocked and I felt bad for unloading all this on her. She didn't deserve this. I felt like I was causing her so much pain and I didn't want to.

"I saw the birthmark mom. It's exactly the same and in the same spot. Jeff is adopted; he never knew who his biological parents were."

My mother stared at Jeff as if seeing him in a new light.

"Yes, your father and I had another child before you were born. It was a baby girl. It was a closed adoption. We wanted her to find a home and leave it up to the new parents to tell her any details. We didn't want to disrupt his life." She looked at him. "I'm sorry. We were so young. We weren't ready."

Jeff nodded. "I understand. I've had a good life as I trust she did, good parents. I always wondered where I came from, but you did nothing wrong in giving your baby daughter up."

My mother looked relieved. It must have been something that weighed heavy on her heart for many years. I had no idea what she must be going through right now. Seeing her perhaps her future son-in-law for the first time in these conditions. It was wrong on so many levels but unfortunately it could not be helped.

"I'm glad to hear that you have had a good life Jeff." My father was back in the conversation, calmer now. He couldn't look me in the eyes however, he was ashamed of me. Ashamed that I had sex so young, had moved out of the family home and had managed to have sex. Never mind I forced my mother to admit her deep dark family secret. Yeah I was starting to feel amazing right at that moment.

"So now we are back to a larger issue. The fact that you two have been carrying on a sexual relationship."

"Yes," I said shamefully.

We all stared at Jeff. We all knew it to be true, he was the only one trying to remain in denial.

"Son, come with me. Let me see the birthmark."

Jeff looked uncomfortable at first but he followed my father out of the room.

I looked at my mother. "I'm sorry mom. I didn't mean to bring up the past."

She looked at me for a long moment. "I think I'm sorrier for you. I'm glad Jeff is here, if he is to become my son-in-law I would like to know him."

She came over to where I was sitting. She put her arms around me and made me feel safe once again. She was always really good at that.

My father and Jeff returned to the room and both looked sombre.

"What did you find Harold?"

"It's the same. I mean it's very close to what mine looks like. When I first became aware of mine, I asked my doctor about it and he told me that each birthmark is unique, that no, birthmarks are not genetic. Birthmarks are, usually, nothing more than irregularities in one's skin present at the time of birth. They are not genetic. It is best, however, to keep an eye on them to ensure that they don't turn cancerous."

I started to cry then and Jeff came to me immediately. "I'm so sorry Carrie that this needlessly upset you."

"Carrie, how could you come here and embarrass the family like this? What were you thinking?"

"Harold back off, she's upset enough already."

I sat up. "Dad this has nothing to do with you and how you feel about this. I came here to find out if my boyfriend is my brother and now that I know, forgive me if I didn't find it a little upsetting."

"The two of you have no business having sex. Carrie you are much too young and we know that Jeff is much older than you are. You should not be having sex and if you weren't, then you wouldn't be in this position."

"Harold, you are just being cruel. Kids have sex, it happens. It's not something you can control."

"Your daughter is incredible Sir. I did not get involved with her on some whim. I care a great deal about her. I would never do anything to hurt her."

"Well you almost did. Now what are the two of you going to do?"

"Dad we are aware of what it all means for us."

"Harold, I think we need to consider all of us going into counselling to get this figured out. These two kids are serious about each other and they almost were given some terrible news. They need to work through it and it sure would be helpful to all of us to get some professional help for this."

"Yes, you are probably right."

"Well I have had enough for one night mom and dad. I need to go home and rest."

Jeff and I got up from the couch and made our way to the door.

"I will look into someone for us to talk to Carrie," My mother offered.

I just nodded. There was nothing left to say. My life had changed drastically and I didn't know how to deal with the fact that I have a sister somewhere and may never get to meet her. I could only be thankful that no one at the office had found out about us. That would have been a scandal that I didn't think I could deal with.

We walked to the car in silence as I tried to understand why this had happened to me.

We drove back to my apartment and stood at the front of my building just staring at each other. It was hard for me to look at Jeff and see anything but the man who had seduced me in so many ways. I loved him I knew that much to be true

"I'm sorry Carrie. Sorrier than you will ever know. What went on between us really meant something to me."

"I know it did. I felt it all too, but you know we can still be together right?"

"I know," he said.

I kissed his mouth and turned away from him quickly. I had to be alone to process everything that has tossed my life around.

Chapter Eleven
Carrie

Being apart from Jeff almost killed me. I never would have thought that I could love someone as much as I loved him. We had collided together in such a way that it was almost magical, there was just no other way to explain it. But just as quickly as we fell in love, we then fell apart.

It had been a month since I last saw Jeff and being apart from him was no easy task. My days were filled with pain and I often wondered if we made the right decision when we separated.

Since our separation Jeff secured me a job as an assistant with another company; a company owned by a friend of his. The pain was extraordinarily good so I could hardly complain. I missed working for Jeff though but we both knew that if I stayed with his company it would have made things very difficult between us. He did however want to make sure that I was taken care of. Despite what we found out about our parents he didn't want me to end up having to depend on them again. I had no intention of moving back home no matter what happened. I was more than happy living with Donna but I had also been thinking lately of getting my own place. I was a grown woman now and it was probably time that I considered trying to make it on my own.

I sipped my coffee thinking about the last conversation I had with Jeff. Walking away from him had been the hardest thing I had ever done. No…that probably wasn't true either. It was much harder not hearing from him after that. I had been through breakups before; usually there was a period of time where you still stayed in contact. That period when you wondered about each other, worried and still missed the other person. But I had not received one text or phone call from Jeff since we walked away from each other. I'm not really sure what I expected since we were in an impossible situation but I expected him to miss me to want to still talk to me. I just wanted some indication that this situation might be hard on him as well. It truly sucked missing him on my own, never truly knowing how he felt about me. Maybe he realized that his feelings weren't really that strong for me and that he had to move on. That would make things easier on him. But it had felt so real, for me anyways but maybe it hadn't felt that way for him.

I couldn't believe that I was in love with my brother. That was the sick reality of my situation. It wasn't something that I planned. One day Jeff was just some guy that walked into the diner that I worked at and saved me. He gave me a better job and a chance at a new life. I certainly hadn't expected to fall in love with my boss but when I did I never regretted it for a moment. The regrets only began after I saw the birth mark. The birth mark that changed everything for the both of us. One day during an intimate moment together we realized that we both shared the same heart shaped birth marks on our bottoms. The only time I had ever seen that same birth mark before was on my father when I accidently walked in on him having sex with my mother. It was scarring for sure. That's when my world started to fall apart. We didn't want to believe it; hell I had wanted to stay in denial as long as possible. But we both knew that Jeff had been adopted and we knew we had to know the truth.

It didn't take long to find it once we talked to my father and found out that he did father a child earlier in life before I was born and that child had been given up for adoption. After a series of tests had been conducted we had found out that indeed he was my brother. After that we didn't know what else to do but breakup. I mean what could we do? We were related. The best we could hope for at that point was to be friends and that would take some time. I wasn't sure if I would ever be able to spend time with him without longing for more. Not that I would be able to avoid him forever, let's be honest he was now part of the family and there were certainly chances of us running into each other at some point. The thought of it turned my stomach.

It was a Saturday and I had the day off. I was still in my nightshirt wondering what I was going to do with my day when there was a knock on the door. I looked at it suspiciously wondering who would just drop by unannounced. It rarely happened but it was likely one of Donna's friends wondering where she was. I got up from the kitchen table and made my way to the door.

My jaw hit the floor when I opened it and found Jeff on the other side looking rather sheepish. My heart started beating furiously in my chest and I thought that I had stopped breathing. We stood there and stared at each other for a moment unsure of who would start speaking first.

"Jeff, what are you doing here?"

"I don't know."

I laughed, "Well that clears everything up."

He chuckled, "Do you mind if I come in for a bit? Nice pj's by the way."

I looked down at my night shirt realizing I was not dressed. I blushed deeply as I looked back up at him. "I wasn't expecting company. It's my day off and you are pretty much the last person I expected to come to my door. But please come in." I motioned for him to come in and he walked by me. I watched him as I closed the door behind me. He went directly into the kitchen and poured himself a cup of coffee.

"By all means, help yourself."

He smiled as he refilled my cup as well. "We need to talk."

"Why? I thought we said everything we needed to each other. What more could we say?"

He sighed, "Carrie, I have been a wreck this past month. You are all I have been thinking about. I don't know what the hell to do but I'm not happy."

"A wreck, really? You could have fooled me. I haven't heard a peep out of you this whole time. In fact I was started to wonder if you forgot about me totally."

He sat down at the table across from me. My hands circled around my cup to keep me warm.

"You can't mean that. How could I ever forget about you Carrie? Be real here."

"So why haven't you call if you were so out of sorts?"

"I haven't called because I didn't know what to say. Cut me some slack here. Things between us are complicated…almost impossible. I didn't know how to fix it or if it should even be fixed. Never mind the fact that our father has been up and down me about staying away from you."

"Dad? Why? What's his problem? He hasn't said a word to me."

"And he probably wouldn't; he thinks it would be one more excuse for you to rebel against him and do what you want."

My anger flared. "Rebel against him? What the hell? How did I rebel? Just because I wanted a life of my own instead of living with them and working at the family diner my whole life? Yeah, I must have been a real tyrant, God forbid I want to do something else with my life." I wasn't sure why I was getting so angry; my father, however, had a way of getting to me like no one else. He had expected me to stay his little mouse all my life and never leave home. I had been part of his 'flock' attending church three times a week and never asking for anything more. I worked at the diner even though I hated every minute of it. He had wanted me to stay in the family business even though my sister had been allowed to move to the city and become a lawyer. But no, he had never wanted anything great for me. When I had taken a stand and moved out on my own and started a real job he had just about lost his mind and disowned me. It had taken a lot for him to speak to me again, something I had to thank Jeff for but it shouldn't have got to that point. I had done nothing wrong. But in his eyes I had done everything wrong because it wasn't his way of doing things.

"Carrie, I know you and your dad have a complicated history and he hasn't been the most understanding person when it came to your life, but he isn't a bad person. He really just wants the best for you and for me as well."

"By telling you to stay away from me? Yeah, that's really helpful."

"Well, look at things from his perspective. He has to explain to all the people in his life that he has a new son in his life, one he gave up for adoption once upon a time because he had a fling with someone. That's bad enough. Now, he has to tell everyone that his new son is going to date his daughter? I don't even think he could handle something like that. He thinks the very idea of us being together is an abomination."

"Yeah, I get it. We broke up remember; you don't think the whole thing blows my mind too? But it's different. We didn't grow up together. I had no idea you even existed. We had sex Jeff and fell in love before I had any idea that you were related to me. It's not our fault."

"Carrie, I know it's not our fault. It's just a messed up situation and I don't know what to do about it."

I took a sip of my coffee. He was right; there was no denying it. The situation we were in was beyond messed up. Yet there I was looking at him across the table and thinking that I never wanted to be away from him. He had been everything to me. He still was, having him sitting across from me I realized that I missed him like crazy and my feelings for him had not changed at all.

"So why are you here then Jeff?"

He looked into his coffee cup for what felt like forever. When he finally looked up at me, there was something in his eyes I just couldn't read. I wondered then if he still loved me.

"I want you Carrie."

Those few words softened me like nothing else could. I wanted him too and yet I wasn't sure I could have him. My father thought we were an abomination. Were we? Wasn't it possible to fall in love with the wrong person but have everything work out anyways? I wanted to believe it.

"What do you want Jeff?"

"I want you Carrie. I love everything about you. Hell, I think I may have even loved you that first day I walked into the diner. You were so beautiful and lonely, you drew me in. There was nothing I wanted more than to take you away from there."

"And you did," I interjected.

"Yes, I did."

"Now what?"

He looked and me and shrugged simply. I couldn't be angry with him because I had no answers myself.

"You're all I think about. The way you talk and the way you smell. Just everything. You are so easy to love. And that body…" He said with a smile.

"Oh and what about my body."

"You are so fuckable. That ass of yours was so ripe for the taking. Thinking about the sex we had together is enough to drive a man wild."

I looked at him and the heat that he had in his eyes. I knew exactly how he was feeling because I had the same heat in my own eyes. I wanted him like I never wanted anything else in my life. I reached for him stretching myself over the table at him and our lips touch in a searing interlude. It was like we had never been apart. It felt perfect and right. How could something that tasted so good be so wrong? I needed him and I was going to take what I wanted.

"Take me Jeff please. I want you so badly. I need you inside me."

He grinned, loving my words and we both stood up from the table and went to each other. His hands were on my ass as we kissed. He lifted me up into his arms and my legs circled his waist. Jeff carried me to my bedroom and laid me down on the bed. All I could think about was what it would feel like to have him inside me and nothing else.

Chapter Twelve

Carrie

Was it possible that my heart was beating even more furiously than it had when I saw him at the door? I thought it was going to burst through my ribcage and come through my chest. *Thump thump thump, oh god I might even pass out.* I had never done anything so brazen before but it was exciting...and a little naughty. There was a part of me that knew that I shouldn't be doing this and yet I had to. I wanted it more than anything. It was just between Jeff and I, no one would ever know that I had embarked on a sexual interlude that was frowned upon, right? Jeff was just a guy who wanted to please me in various ways, what was wrong with that? I grew warm all over with the thought, I was actually becoming incredibly horny as his tongue continued to play with my own.

He just stared at me, I could tell he was feeling exactly the same way that I was. He wanted me and I remembered what he said about what sex was like between us. God that turned me on so much. He was so right; we literally caught on fire together. How many positions would it be this time? What was he about to do to me? Would I like it, would I want more of it? Beg for it? When it came to Jeff, nothing was off the table. I already knew that much.

"So, what should we do first?"

He flashed me a devilish grin that made me warm all over. "I'm going to make you feel really good Carrie by doing dirty things to you."

I gasped; no one had ever talked that way to me before I knew Jeff and I have had some pretty darn good sex in my day. Why had no one done it before? It hadn't even occurred to me to request it or need it but I certainly liked it now. I couldn't get enough of it. Ever since I had met Jeff he had talked to me in that manner and it was intoxicating.

He leaned in and slipped his hand around my neck pulling me in to him as his mouth claimed mine. He tasted sweet and alluring. His mouth was hot to the touch and I almost moaned at his touch. He kissed me softly at first and then his kisses became more fevered as if he needed my mouth on his. His tongue slipped into my mouth and I claimed it. I sucked him slowly; tasting him before I pulled away. He pulled me in again as he was not finished kissing me. His tongue found mine again and our kisses grew more passionate. His hand found my breast and he kneaded it softly. He began pulling off my night shirt and tossing it aside. I didn't have a bra on so there was no worry of that. He stopped kissing me momentarily to look down at my breasts.

"You are so beautiful."

I smiled though all I could think about was what he looked like naked. His mouth found my nipple and he sucked, nipped and licked it. The sensation I was getting was making my panties wet. I moaned softly as he replaced his mouth with his fingers and pulled on my nipple causing an ache between my legs. I liked it, it made me horny. He continued playing with my nipples causing me to moan as a pleasure built up in my body. My hand reached down and I massaged the front of his pants, I could feel his hard cock pushing against his pants. Jeff smiled down at me. "Do you want it? Do you want it in your mouth?"

I nodded, still speechless by the things that came out of his mouth. I felt wanton around him, like I would do just about anything for pleasure. To have him please my body, to give me what I wanted. He undid his button and pulled the zipper on his pants down. He brought his pants down to his knees and slid his underwear down with them. His hard cock bounced before me now free from his underwear. Jeff was so big; the sight was always breathtaking to me. I sat up on the bed as he stood in front of me. I took his cock into my mouth and sucked on it. His eyes closed above me and I sucked hard while I massaged his balls. My tongue began to swirl against his shaft and then around his tip. He moaned with eagerness and I sucked him even harder.

"Oh god, you're good at this Carrie."

I took his cock deeper into my mouth until it hit the back of my throat. I moved up and down rhythmically until I moved fluidly with him in my mouth.

His moans excited me and I felt my pussy become very wet. He pulled his cock out of my mouth and finished undressing himself. I slid out of my panties. He watched me undress and he couldn't take his eyes off my pussy.

"Mmm, you look good. Maybe good enough to eat. I want to stick my tongue inside of you."

I didn't hesitate to lean back in the chair and spread my legs. I wanted him between my legs; I wanted him to lick my pussy. Having his tongue inside me excited me incredibly.

Jeff dropped down before me and licked my pussy slowly as if he was licking an ice cream cone on a hot summer day. It felt incredible as his tongue licked the sides of my opening, causing a tingle to run through my body. He took my clit in his mouth and sucked on it causing me to moan loudly as my pussy dripped.

"Oh god...oh god...Jeff"

He looked up and smiled, "Does that feel good baby?"

"Oh god yes, it feels incredible."

My pussy was dripping and he was licking it up tasting every inch of me. I felt the buildup coming. I was going to cum right there.

"Oh god, oh wow, I'm going to cum."

Jeff was sucking on my clit when he buried a finger inside my pussy and started pumping away. It was too much, too much all at once and I cried out softly as I had an orgasm so delicious that I wanted even more. I wanted to be fucked multiple times. I didn't want it to ever end.

"How was that?"

I just grinned with desire written all over my face.

"Let me sit down baby. I want you to sit on my cock and ride it."

He sat down on the bed while I stood up. I grinned loving the sound of his words. I got into position with my back facing him and plunged myself onto his cock. He was pushed right up against my g-spot in that position and the feeling made me just about lose my mind. He was so deep and hard it was like he was touching every nerve inside of me.

I was rendered speechless and I started moving slowly. He felt fantastic and I started riding his smooth cock even harder. He was moaning softly as well and it was making me lose control.

"Mmmm, you sexy girl. You feel delicious. You ride my cock good baby. Keep going."

I moaned, his voice, his words, his cock was driving me mad. And just when I thought it couldn't get any better he reached around and started playing with my clit. It was almost too much to bear, I couldn't get enough. I was moaning softly wanting to beg for more but feeling already possessed by him. My pussy was so wet, he was driving me wild.

"Just relax sweetheart." I gasped as pleasure coursed through to me. I continued pumping onto his cock as an orgasm took a hold of me once again. "Oh god Jeff, oh god that feels so good," I whispered my yearnings to him.

"I want to put my cock in you and fuck you. It's my turn. Let's switch again."

I lifted myself off his cock and waited to see what he had in mind.

His cock, oh god, looking at his size made me horny all over again. I wanted to be fucked by him desperately.

I couldn't believe all that was happening. It was hard to believe I was in that situation, right there in my room with a man I had no business being with and I loved every moment of it. How could I ever say no to him? He caused my body to throb immensely until I wanted to beg him to release me from that feeling. I needed him at that point, to fuck me so that I would get the release that I wanted, the release that I deserved. I wanted to be fucked over and over again by that man. This was the kind of therapy one needs after a tough day at the office, screw therapy, or wine or hot baths, the way to feel better was to be fucked properly.

He got up from the bed and pushed me down on it again. I lay out on the bed and when he pushed my legs up over my head my eyes widened. Thank god, I was flexible. I wondered what he planned on doing to me.

I did as I was told, my body weakened from pleasure. I was lying on my back, my legs spread before him and above him.

"Touch yourself for me."

My eyes popped open. I shook my head, "Jeff, I can't. I don't know how."

"Yes, you can. I want to see you please yourself it turns me on and then I'm going to slide inside that wet pussy of yours and fuck you really good."

Nervousness swelled inside my stomach, I had masturbated before, obviously, but never in front of anyone. So I did what any sane woman would do and I spread my legs and slid my fingers through the wetness that was all over my pussy. I swirled it around before moving up to my clit, massaging it with my finger. I grinded into it, closing my eyes as I enjoyed my own touch. I was sure my face was a bright crimson but he didn't say a thing. In fact when I opened my eyes he was staring down at me mesmerized by what I was doing. He looked up at me with fire in his eyes and the look on his face made me feel incredible; like I was completely in control of his pleasure. I loved the feeling of controlling his lust and I inserted two fingers inside my pussy and moaned as they went in deep. I finger fucked myself in front of him watching a slow smile form on his face.

"That is so hot Carrie."

I moaned as I pleasured myself, taking my fingers out and swirling my juices around my clit. I was throbbing all over and I desperately wanted to be fucked at that point.

"Please?"

"Please what darling, do you want some help?"

"I want you."

"Then you can have me." He positioned himself in the missionary position and put my legs up over my head again. He entered me slowly and I gasped with how deep he went.

"Oh yes, this is nice. You're nice and tight baby. God your pussy feels so good." The level of deepness in that position was crazy good.

I leaned my head back, delirious with pleasure. He fit inside me perfectly and I got a wave of pleasure every time Jeff moved inside me. He began pumping me a little faster, causing me to moan loudly. His cock was perfect and with the position we were using, he was in the perfect spot to hit my G-spot over and over again. My body built up once again and I knew that he was going to cause me to cum all over his cock.

"Cum for me baby, I can see it on your face. Cum all over my cock."

I exploded then doing as he asked, screaming loudly. I was spent and yet he kept fucking me slowly. He pulled out and pulled me off the bed. I followed him around my bed and he told me to lie down on the floor. I quickly looked at the door and was amazed that we had not been discovered at that point by Donna. Not that she would just walk into my bedroom unannounced but she was due home shortly and who knows what kind of noise we were making at that point.

"You have such a nice ass; you should see this glorious view that I have."

Jeff slid inside my pussy hard. I cried out as pleasure over took my body. I was on my back but he positioned me so that his hands grasped under my ass and he lifted me up and supported my weight. The only think on the ground were my shoulders and I wrapped my legs around his waist. I moaned, enjoying every inch of his cock as he pounded me over and over again. He leaned down towards me and spanked my ass. I cried out realizing I had never experienced anything so sexy in my entire life. He pumped into me harder waves of pleasure rolling off of me. I smiled up at him and stifled my moans as best I could as another orgasm ripped through me. I was having multiple orgasms with this man, how was I ever to return to normal sex again?

"You have a real nice pussy Carrie, I like fucking you."

I moaned, loving the way he was making me feel, but even more so by the way he talked to me.

He pulled out again and laid me down gently on the floor. He slid his fingers into my pussy and finger fucked me for a bit, he was making me wet all over again, although at that point I was pretty soaked from all the fucking. "I want you back on my cock baby, will you sit on me again and ride me good."

"You bet your ass I will."

He returned to the bed and sat himself on the edge of it. All these different positions were exciting. There was never a dull moment with Jeff that much was certainly true. I positioned myself so I had my back to him again and slid his cock inside me. My eyes fluttered closed when I did so.

"There we go darling; we are going to go easy. That feels good doesn't it?" I moaned in agreement.

"Okay, here we go, just stay relaxed, don't tense up."

I could hardly believe myself at that moment what had ever possessed me to do such a thing, having sex with Jeff again? We had agreed that we could not be together, that it was just not going to work, so what were we doing? God, I had wanted him so badly, I still did. I was so sexually satisfied but yet so horny still I would have let him do just about anything to me. I was aching inside with want of him. I had never thought of having sex like this before; it just never occurred to me to try such a thing. I hadn't realized the pleasure that could be brought to me by such a man. Jeff just wanted to bring as much pleasure to my body as I could stand.

I rode Jeff's cock feeling the delicious sensations spread all over my body.

"Just relax sweetheart, you are tensing up. I can feel you hugging my cock."

I hadn't realized that I was holding my breath so I did as he said. As I pushed onto him a little more, I tried to relax and allowed it to happen. He certainly felt huge when he was going in on this end. I felt full with him in my pussy, but I loved every moment of it. He then began to move his hips and meet my thrusts onto his cock. He was trying to allow me to get used to more inside of me. I moaned as he picked up the pace, his smooth cock gliding inside and out.

"Are you okay baby?"

"Yes," I whispered.

"Does it feel good?"

"God yes Jeff. I love learning new positions with you."

The thought of having a variety of positions available to me had never occurred to me but it sounded like a hot idea and it was one of the things that I like most about our sex life. Riding on him he felt humongous inside me. Jeff rocked into me slowly continuing to meet my thrusts. I started rocking into him faster letting the waves of pleasure crash into me repeatedly, not much break in between.

"Oh god," I moaned.

He reached around and felt for my pussy. He rubbed against my moist clit giving me some added pleasure while he moved his cock inside me.

"Okay baby, I want you to fuck me good."

I thought I would lose my mind with the words coming out of his mouth. He was so sexy and experienced and he was showing me a world I had never thought existed. Or one that I at least never imagined I would venture into.

The whole length of his cock slowly pushed inside me causing me to let out a slow and powerful moan. There were so many different feelings and sensations going through my body at that moment. I was lost in a sea of pleasure and I wanted to let go of another orgasm.

"I want more."

I heard him chuckle and he started pumping me as I thrust onto him. I was delirious with the pleasure he was giving me, I needed it, needed him.

What I didn't expect was for my pussy to become so wet. I was dripping wet and I felt a buildup once again. I couldn't believe I was about to cum again. God, the thought was just too delicious.

"Jeff, it feels so good baby. It really does feel so good."

"I know Carrie. It's amazing isn't it?"

"Yes," I gasped, "I'm coming again."

My whole body shuddered as I came on his cock. He continued pumping inside of me, breaking all reason inside my mind. He was glorious; all of it was so incredible. The best sex of my life was happening with my brother. As I felt myself build up for another orgasm, the shudders ripped through my body causing me to ache to scream his name.

"Oh Carrie, I'm ready too baby. I'm going to fill up your pussy with cum."

I moaned loving how sexy he was with his dirty talk. He spilled inside of me and collapsed against my bed.

I slid slowly off his cock and I knew for certain that I was going to be very sore the next day. It would have all been worth it though. I dug around in my side table and pulled out some Kleenex's and handed them to him. I cleaned myself off as best that I could and slipped into my panties. I slipped into my night shirt again as I watched him rummaging around for his clothes that had fallen to the floor. Finding them he quickly slipped into underwear and jeans, pulling his t-shirt over his head.

"So that certainly cleared up our problem, didn't it?"

I looked up at him as reality hit home once again. I couldn't seem to wipe the grin off my face though, so maybe it wasn't the end of the world. My hands shook from the toile the orgasms took on my body. Jeff was watching me and when I looked up at him he smiled. He had a stunner of a smile and the look of him made me want to start all over again. Would I ever be able to get enough of that man or was it always going to be this way? God, I hoped it was.

"I don't want to lose you Jeff." I giggled as I pulled him in for another deep kiss.

"Maybe we should go and get some food and talk about it?"

I nodded though I was sad to have the sex end. What great memories there were in this room that was for sure.

Jeff spanked my ass softly and said, "I'm not sure how you're going to explain your hair but let's get you out of here."

Chapter Thirteen
Jeff

I think it became rather obvious to Carrie quickly on that I had no intention of talking to her about our situation once we arrived at the bar. I had left her at the apartment and told her to get ready and I would pick her up that evening. I had planned on talking to her about us but as the day waned on the thought of it gave me a touch of anxiety. I had no idea what I was going to do about our situation. I didn't want to anger the father I had finally found after 30 years but I also didn't want to lose Carrie. Though when it came to Carrie, I wasn't even sure that I had a right to put a claim on her; she was my sister, she wasn't meant to be mine.

"What are we doing? I thought we were going out for dinner?"

"Change of plans. I say we have some fun for a change."

"Jeff...seriously this isn't going to go away."

"It will for tonight. Come on."

I took her up to the bar and we sat down on some stools. Aside from the private booths in the VIP area it seemed to be the only seating in the entire establishment. There were a good mix of men and women in the club and they seemed to be having a raucous time. I often came to this club especially back when I was a bachelor. I guess I was still a bachelor since things between Carrie and I had stalled. It was a great place to meet women and the VIP area was stellar.

"So my beauty, what would you like to drink?"

"How about a White Russian?" She was such a pretty girl that it hurt to look at her. I wanted her to be mine. As soon as we walked into the bar all the eyes were on her. I wanted her all to myself but I wasn't sure if that would ever be possible.

"I'm kind of surprised by your choice, but you can have whatever you would like."

She winked at me and I felt myself grow hard. I glanced around the bar wondering if there was some place I could take her for a quickie. Would she let me take her in a bar? That thought intrigued me.

I ordered us up some drinks. The bartender was efficient and I tipped his excessively. I knew he would be at my beck and call for the entire evening now.

I handed her the drink and watched her take a sip. "It's delicious Jeff, thank you."

"You're welcome."

"So tell me something Carrie…"

Her eyebrows rose, "What's that?"

"What the hell are we going to do? I mean I don't want to get into a big debate right now. But just off the top of your head, is there anything that could fix this?"

"Counselling."

She said it quickly and in a no-nonsense sort of way. It was as if she had been thinking about it for some time now. I wondered if she had planned on talking to me long before I came to her apartment. She took another sip of her drink.

"Counselling?"

"Yes, it's pretty simple. We go there and hash it out. If the counsellor thinks we are half mad for trying it, then we give up. If it's the opposite however, then at least we have backup against our father."

"Is that right?" I had to admit that I was surprised that she had come up with a plan already. And it made sense. I wasn't sure what a counsellor would have to say about our unique situation or whether he would throw us through the door for our perversion, but I had to admit that I was curious about what would be said about our situation.

She shrugged sheepishly. She had always been straightforward with me; I had to admire that.

88

"So now you know my thoughts, what do you think?" She took another sip of her White Russian while she watched me. She was looking for some confirmation that she had not totally lost her mind with her idea.

I nodded. I wasn't quite sure what to say to her. There was no point in lying to her; I had to be just as straight forward with her as she had been with me.

"The first time I saw you Carrie, I thought you were breathtaking. I still do. The best part of my day was when you used to walk into my office. I don't normally go after my employees, but with you things were different. They always have been. I'm not sure why I was so drawn to you if we weren't meant to be together. There are a lot of things about this situation that I just don't understand. But I cared a great deal about you."

"So you have said before. What do you think of my idea?"

"I say we go for it. See what they have to say and go from there. It sounds reasonable enough."

She smiled and I hoped that I could keep that small on her face long term.

"What do you say we go do some dancing?" I asked.

She nodded and at least it would get us off the subject for now. I had a lot of thinking to do. But right now all I wanted was to get close to her again.

We got up from our seats and we headed to the dance floor. There were quite a few people already on the dance floor. I wanted Carrie all to myself and the dance floor was the perfect place to put my hands on her. When we arrived to the middle of the dance floor I grabbed her by the waist and pulled her into my body. Having her so close caused my body to go warm all over. There was just some-thing so captivating about her, she drew me in. She had beautiful blue eyes and I got lost in them.

I brushed the hair out of Carrie's face and pressed her tightly against me. She smiled and it turned me on that much more. I bent down and nipped her neck with my teeth. She gasped and giggled up at me. I felt aggressive with her in my arms and I wished I had a place that I could take her and ravage her. My hands found her hips and I held her to me. I grew hard with her in my arms and I could tell by the surprised look on her face that she felt it to. I was surprised myself that I could get turned on just by dancing with Carrie, but she seemed to have that effect on me. We were so close at that point that we could be one person. The music pounded around us and I could only breathe her in. I wondered how wise it would be for me to kiss her at that moment. Would it just drag us in deeper before we knew if it was the right thing to do?

"Do you have any idea what we are getting into here Carrie?"

"I'm aware of your dark side Jeff. I don't care. I want to be with you."

I laughed. I wanted it too but I just wondered if we were kidding ourselves.

I was close to her face feeling like a little insane. That was what it was like being close to her and not touching her. I no longer cared about anything or who else was in the room. It felt like it was just the two of us. I wanted to possess her mind and body.

Chapter Fourteen

Carrie

"Come, I need you." Jeff grabbed me and pulled me off the dance floor. My heart was beating fast and I longed to be close to him once again. He held my hand as he led me through the crowd and up a grand staircase. He was leading me to the VIP lounge and I wondered what he had in store for me. He spoke briefly with one of the hosts and I realized that he was securing us with a booth. With enough money you could get anything you want, even at the last minute. Some of the booths had privacy curtains on them in case you didn't want to be interrupted by other guests. There were a few other groups up there that were having their own parties.

Jeff took me to one of the private booths and we went inside. They were roomy and elegant. It was practically big enough for me to sleep in.

"These are some impressive booths."

"Yeah, they are nice aren't they?"

A waitress then peeked inside our booth and smiled at us. "Hi there. What can I get for you two?"

The waitress had raven black hair and a bust I would kill for. I couldn't keep my eyes off of her and yet Jeff barely paid her any attention. It was refreshing to see that Jeff wasn't ogling the girl.

He looked up at her. "Absolutely. Can you bring us a bottle of Bollinger Blanc de Noirs? Actually bring us two bottles."

My eyebrows rose again. I had never heard of those brands but the fact that he ordered a specific one told me they were probably very expensive. Not only that, but two? The waitress looked at him with interest and I rolled my eyes. I wasn't going to complain however, why not get drunk with my brother, whom I was in love with, on expensive champagne?" Did he always order like this when he was out?

"I will get that right away for you sir." She left us alone and I smiled at Jeff.

"I think she fell in love with you when you ordered? You know you don't have to try to impress me. I'm already smitten with you."

He chuckled. "Yeah, well the feeling is mutual. I like fine things Carrie; you should know that by now. Let's live a little."

I loved listening to Jeff talk. He was a smart man and that was important to me.

"So how do you like the new company?"

"It's great, everyone there is so nice. I really appreciate you making sure that I got a good job."

"Of course. What else was I supposed to do? I finally did something nice for you and then ruined it by getting involved with you."

"It was my choice too Jeff. I wanted to be with you. I just didn't expect us to break up and it all fall apart."

"I know and if it means anything to you, I didn't expect it either. It was the last thing I ever expected to happen. I just wanted to make sure that you were okay after. Do you miss working for me?"

"Of course I do. I loved working with you and I wish that I still did."

"Maybe one day we can change all that."

"Maybe." I said with a smile.

The waitress came back with a bucket full of ice and two champagne bottles. She set down a couple of flutes for us and poured us each a glass. My mouth was literally watering as I imagined what the champagne would taste like. What a treat it would be to have some expensive champagne.

"Thank you so much. I don't want to be disturbed for a while however. If we need anything else I will come and fetch you." She nodded, though she looked disappointed. Jeff slipped her a hundred dollar bill and she disappeared.

"So what should we toast to?"

"How about the counsellor not throwing us out of her office?"

He laughed. "You're hilarious."

I sighed, "Okay let's toast to second chances."

"That sounds perfect."

I picked up my glass and we clinked them together. I brought the glass to my lips and took a tentative sip. The taste was crisp and smooth. It was the most delicious liquid ever to go down my throat.

"God, that's good." I said with a giggle.

"You have no idea."

He surprised me with a kiss. His mouth met my lips and the heat just ignited between us. I moaned underneath his lips.

"I can taste the champagne on your lips Carrie." He said with a smile.

Everything that came out of Jeff's mouth was hot. I could taste the champagne on his lips as well and I liked the combination of the sweetness of the champagne and his musky taste.

We kissed again and our tongues found each other. We started making out like we were in high school. As our kisses became more heated, his hands were in my hair.

He stood up and lifted me up. I giggled as he took me in his arms. I wondered if people outside of the curtain could hear us. He lifted me onto the table and moved in between my legs. I was so incredibly turned on, I wasn't sure what Jeff had in mind but I was up for anything. I didn't care; I was going to allow Jeff to take me wherever he wanted. My mind was racing as I watched him zip down his pants. Was he going to fuck me right there in the middle of the booth? I couldn't possibly believe what was happening between us and yet it all felt so natural. I wasn't sure if this was the right thing to do and I wondered about what was going to happen to Jeff and me. My thoughts suddenly shut down when he dropped his pants and then his underwear. I gasped at his forwardness. When our eyes met he smiled and I couldn't help but smile back. I couldn't believe I was about to be fucked in a luxury booth but it was surprisingly liberating to think about it. I had zero issue with what was about to happen to me. The moment couldn't have been sexier and I spread my legs wide for him. His cock was hard and it stood up ready for me. I fumbled with my dress but Jeff stopped me. "What?" I asked.

"I want to fuck you with that dress on." He pushed up the skirt portion of my dress and revealed my lace panties. He slid aside my panties and felt my pussy with his hand. I had already grown wet with anticipation; I couldn't have been more excited to have him so close to me. I could see his cock and I ached for it. I needed him badly and just seeing his cock bob before me was enough to get me very excited.

"Your pussy feels nice Carrie, you're so wet." I moaned as he pushed a finger inside my pussy and finger fucked me. My eyes fluttered. God that felt so good. I couldn't believe what was happening to me. I couldn't even think straight while he was touching me. Was I really going to let him fuck me right there at the club? I smiled as I thought about it. Yes, I was, I was going to let Jeff fuck me on the table. Hopefully, he would fuck me really good. Who was I kidding? Of course he was going to fuck me good. Look at the man; he was built to fuck me good. "Mmmm, that feels so good Jeff."

I smiled and crushed his mouth with a kiss searching out his tongue, sucking on it. He moaned and the sound thrilled me. I loved pleasing him and I wanted to do more of it. I wanted to taste every inch of him but we didn't exactly have the room for it. I needed his cock, though, and I was going to enjoy every minute of it. He continued to kiss me as he finger fucked me and I was bombarded with waves of pleasure from his fingers as I enjoyed his kisses. I moved in and kissed Jeff passionately as he fucked me.

He took his fingers out of me and put his hands on my bottom and squeezed it tight. I loved feeling his hands on me; it felt amazing. I couldn't believe how turned on I was by his touch. I kissed his jaw-line, nipping at his throat. He growled and I bit him even harder. My hands found his cock as I played with his balls before bending down. I didn't have a lot of room but I wasn't missing the opportunity to taste his cock; I wanted it in my mouth badly. It looked incredible before me and I ached to have it in my mouth. I bent down and took his cock into my mouth.

Jeff let out a long moan as his hands were lost in my hair. I sucked hard while massaging his balls. I loved the power that I had when his cock was in my mouth. I controlled the pleasure that he got in that moment. His cock hit the back of my throat and he called out my name. Hearing him say the word Carrie sounded so wonderful. It was more of a growl and it was just what I needed to make me very wet. I moved in rhythm over his cock starting off slow then picking up the pace. My mouth moved onto his cock slowly at first and then his cock pounded into my mouth. I didn't want to make him cum right away so I kept slowing things down.

"God, Carrie that feels incredible. Wow, that is so good."

I continued to suck him twirling my tongue around his tip. His cock was hard in my mouth and taking it in brought me so much pleasure. I could feel myself getting wet all over again.

"Darling, I need to be inside you. Carrie, I'm going to fuck you so good. I can't wait to give you my cock."

I slid him out of my mouth gently as he pushed me back onto the table. There was a fire in his eyes and I knew I was in for a night to remember. I lay back down onto the table, spreading my legs for him. He looked at my pussy as if he was falling in love with it and he climbed on top of me lifting my dress to take a look. Jeff pulled down my panties and slid a finger inside me once again. He finger fucked me fast enjoying the look of ecstasy that came over my face.

"Oh god...Jeff come inside me, please. I want you so badly. Fuck me good." I marvelled at the fact that I was doing something I never would have considered before but things with Jeff seemed normal, that it shouldn't be any other way. I was more than happy to be fucked by Jeff; in fact I was aching to have his cock inside me. I couldn't wait any longer.

Resting my feet on his shoulders, he plunged deep inside me. I gasped as the full length of his cock went inside me, pumping in and out. I called out his name which drove him mad. Wow, everything about this man was incredible. Everything that I could ask for in a man. It occurred to me that the other guests could hear us fucking. I dismissed the thought instantly however, the music in the club was so loud that most people couldn't hear each other talk. I was confident that no one could hear how much I was enjoying being fucked by Jeff.

"Your pussy feels amazing Carrie. I can't get enough of you. What a nice tight pussy you have."

I could barely think as waves of pleasure washed over me continuously. I had lost all ability to think and reason. I only saw him, felt him and I had never felt so complete in my life. I felt a tension build up inside of me and I came on his cock, releasing an orgasm so strong it rocked my body. He came soon after and he fell exhausted onto my chest. I kissed his head gently putting my fingers through his hair. I felt so satisfied I could have fallen asleep right then and there. I would not however fall asleep in a club booth. I had my limits.

"That was amazing." Jeff murmured.

I smiled, "I'd say. Champagne and sex. Well thank you very much Jeff. Talk about a night to remember."

He chuckled. "I'm glad you enjoyed it. Shall we finish that champagne?"

"I would love to." I said smiling broadly.

He pulled out of me and handed me some napkins. I cleaned myself off and slipped back into my panties. I slid off the table and pulled down my dress. I felt so satisfied. I sat down beside him in the booth once again and I couldn't wipe the smile off my face. He was a handsome man, complicated, but handsome. I had no regrets about what we just did. He filled up our glasses once again and I took a sip. It tasted even better now than it did before we had sex.

Chapter Fifteen

Jeff

I awoke the next morning and rolled over to find the beautiful Carrie looking rumpled, her head upon her pillow. Even though my morning felt like perfection, I felt dread in my belly. I had no idea if I could keep her to myself or if I would lose her forever. We had a plan but there were no guarantees with it. In fact, it could completely blow up in our faces.

As I watched her, her eyes fluttered open and she smiled warmly at me. If only it were that easy. I had found the perfect woman but she ended up being my sister. You couldn't write this stuff if you wanted to.

I just stared at her as her blue eyes bore into mine. I smiled softly knowing that I was going to take her again. I wanted to ravish her right then but I wasn't sure if she wanted me to. We were getting deeper and deeper before we even knew if it would work. All I could think about however was sliding inside of her.

She sat up then and made the decision for me. She bore her mouth onto mine and the fire that ignited between us was hot as hell. She gasped inside my mouth and my loins burned for her. My hands went into her hair, pulling her closer to me. I felt like I would die without her. I kissed her deeply finding her tongue and sucking on it gently. She moaned and the sounds she made caused me to go rock hard. I needed to hear her moan all day long. I sat up then and pulled her body to mine. I kissed down to her chin and trailed kisses down her neck sucking on her. Her hands found the bulge in my underwear, rubbing me hard, causing a friction that drove me insane. The knowledge that she was eager for my cock drove me half mad. I pulled off her t-shirt and watched as her breasts dropped deliciously before me. I bent down to suck on her pretty pink nipples. She gave a guttural moan and I sucked even harder. She pushed me away; I glimpsed a pair of white lace panties before she slid them to the floor.

"Please Jeff I want you inside me."

I never wanted a lady to beg, I would give her exactly what she wanted. I pulled her up from the bed and turned her over. She gasped in excitement as she bent over for me, her tight round bottom in my face. I bent down and kissed her bottom, moving in real close to her. I was rock hard and I couldn't wait to plunge inside her pink little pussy. Her tight bottom drove me insane and I drove deep inside her causing her to moan loudly. She was tight and wet and I really had to control myself or I would lose myself completely inside her.

"Jeff I need it."

Her ass looked glorious right before me as I plunged deeper inside and moved within her. She called out to me loudly and she came against my cock. I continued to rock inside her and I got my finger very wet from her pussy and slowly inserted it into her bum being careful that I was gentle. She couldn't hold back she cried out in pleasure and I pumped her little ass over and over again. I loved looking at her in the throes of passion. I continued to fuck her as I fingered her ass. I pumped inside her hard and she screamed out as she orgasmed. I had her alright and I made her come over and over again as I fucked her with an intensity she would not soon forget. I finally spilled into her and we lay together in the bed spent. I rolled over to her and kissed her deeply on the mouth.

"I am completely addicted to you Carrie; whatever am I going to do with you?"

"Anything you want Jeff, anything you want."

I grinned. We would be meeting with the counsellor that day. That would be the moment of truth. We would know after spilling our guts about our relationship whether we would be able to make a go of things.

She must have been able to read my mind because she asked, "Are you scared?"

I turned to her. "Yes, I am."

"Everything is going to be okay. I just know it."

I bent over and kissed her softly on the mouth. God, I sure hoped that she was right.

Chapter Sixteen
Carrie

The woman that stared back at us from an office lounge chair could have been anorexic she was so thin and lith. She could have been a ballerina in another life. The first thing I thought of when I saw her was I should have brought in hamburgers with me. We could have all got a good meal in us. The woman was thinner than I was and it kind of angered me. I had a nice trim body but hers was something to be in awe of. I had always thought how graceful ballerinas looked while on stage. Their tight little bodies moving flawlessly across the stage.

I had no idea whether our new counsellor was an anorexic or not, but I could tell that Jeff was admiring her figure in his own way. I rolled my eyes without meaning too. What was it with men and skinny women? Not that I had anything to worry about, I had a curvaceous figure and Jeff adored everything about me. I was one hell of a lucky girl. In fact looking at him sitting on the couch beside me I couldn't help looking forward to getting him home to bed.

This was our first counselling session with Dr. Elizabeth Buckley since we had decided to become a couple and I had to admit that I was nervous about it. I had no idea what this woman would think of us or if she would even be able to help us. I worried that we would end up in the same position we were before, breaking up because the people around us felt we shouldn't be together. I wanted to somehow make things work between us but the odds were already against us so the future seemed uncertain.

"So Carrie and Jeff, I read through a little bit of the profile information that you provided to me when you signed up, but I was wondering if you wouldn't run me through quickly why you feel you need to be here."

I cleared my throat. "Well to be honest with you, I'm not sure if we do need to be here. It's been recommended by our parents and at this point we aren't sure how to begin life as a couple in the situation we find ourselves in."

Dr. Buckley nodded as she skimmed our profile. She knew our situation but I couldn't read her at all. She gave nothing away with her expressions. They were very neutral and empathetic. I had no idea what she thought of us, but I felt no judgment sitting there, in fact I even felt like she might understand what we were going through.

"And what situation would that be."

I paused, a little annoyed since she only wanted me to repeat what she already knew. Well so be it, someone had to do it as so far Jeff had become mute. I glared at him and he shot back a nervous smile.

"Jeff and I are actually…step-siblings. We had no idea of course when we met and engaged in a sexual relationship. We proceeded to fall in love and begin a life as a couple when I found out that Jeff was in fact adopted. I realized this when both Jeff and I use either hand, sometimes both simultaneously, when doing something. Like when we have sex."

Dr. Buckley raised an eyebrow but that was it. She motioned for me to continue.

"It came as quite a shock to us, realizing that we shared the same rare trait. The first time I had seen true ambidexterity was with my father when I walked in on him and my mother having sex. We then approached my parents and found out that my mother had engaged in a previous relationship with another man and conceived Jeff, who was then given up for adoption."

"And how did your parents react to finding out that your boyfriend was in fact your stepbrother?"

"Well they reacted the same as anyone would think. I think my mother almost passed out and my father wanted to strangle me. He already disapproved of my life, so finding out I slept with his stepson didn't actually go over well. He insisted we go to counselling to repair the damage we had done and then he forbade us to be together. We actually broke up for a period of time, my father continued to tell Jeff to stay away from me, but we eventually got back together. And here we are."

Dr. Buckley nodded. "So you two want to remain a couple but you aren't sure you can make it work with all the pressure around you."

"Yes, we were hoping to have a professional opinion that we could bring back to our parents in the hopes of swaying them to allow us to be together."

"What is their status right now?"

Jeff stepped into the conversation allowing me to have a bit of a breather. I was quickly becoming overwhelmed and I hoped to god that the session was going to get easier.

"My stepfather wants to get to know me better obviously. Now that he has me in his life he would like the father/son relationship he missed out on all this time. That's kind of hard to do when his daughter is at the same dining room table playing footsies with me underneath. It makes my father uncomfortable to think of us together in the current situation."

"Why is that?"

"Well he's a very traditional and religious man. The idea of us dating is blasphemous to him, even if we aren't full siblings, so to speak. It would be hard for him to parade his new son around and then people find out that his new son is also dating his daughter…it could make for some uncomfortable conversations. Plus he thinks that it is illegal."

"Yes, I can see why that might be. How does that make you feel?"

"Like shit. I want very much to be a part of my stepfather's life and to get to know him. My adoptive father was wonderful; I couldn't have asked for a better role model but he could never replace my stepfather."

"How do you feel about Carrie? Would you be okay to have her as just your sister?"

I turned to him and watched him. He turned to look at me as well and I saw his expression soften before my eyes. I knew he loved me but that didn't make this situation any easier for him.

"No, I don't think I would be. I've already tried to let go of Carrie and it almost killed me. I love her; I have no doubt in my mind about that. I don't want to lose her but I just don't know how to make it work. Do we have to cut ties with our family?"

I could see the alarm springing up in his face. Cutting ties with my family would be easy for me to do. They had given up on me once already. I had drifted from my father's flock and he had practically disowned me. My mother had barely defended me and it wasn't until I got a good job and proved them wrong that they welcomed me back into the fold again. But now they had their ultimatums out again and at that point I was willing to turn my back on them if it meant making things work with Jeff. I was willing to do that. But things were a little harder for Jeff. He had always gotten along famously with his adoptive parents, and he wanted to do the same with his stepfather and biological mother. He didn't want to have to choose but I felt like that was what it was going to come down to whether he liked it or not. My father wasn't the type to go against his beliefs and I hoped if Jeff had to choose again that he would choose me this time.

"It may come to that Jeff; it all depends on what you want. I know you both came here hoping I would write you some kind of permission slip you could bring home to your parents to get yourself off the hook. But I'm afraid that's not the way it works."

"So, how does it work?" I asked. I looked at Jeff anxiously and he grabbed my hand in his.

"Well it's a good thing for you and Jeff to be here, to discuss how you feel as a couple and to formulate a plan to get you through the hard times. As far as legalities go, since you were raised in different households, there would be no problem with your living together or getting married. As far as your family goes however, it's not going to matter what my opinion is on your situation. It doesn't really matter whether I think what you are doing is right or wrong.

What matters is what your entire family thinks. It is very difficult to challenge someone's religious beliefs with your popular opinion. I don't think he would care what I had to say."

"So what are we to do then? We are in quite a mess but we don't want to give up."

I felt a panic attack creeping up on the sidelines of my mind. I thought the counsellor had been the answer to our problem. But if she couldn't help us then I wasn't sure what we would do. The very thought of having to deal with the situation on our own brought me no small amount of anxiety.

"It's obvious to me that you both care a great deal about each other. So may I offer you a suggestion?"

"Yes of course," Jeff and I said together.

"Move away."

Startled, I wasn't sure how to respond at first. I looked to Jeff whose brow was furrowed in confusion. "What do you mean, move away?"

"As I see it the only way the two of you can make this work is if you live away from your parents, from your family. It's obvious your father doesn't want to see you together as a couple, yet the two of you are determined to stay a couple. So my suggestion to you would be to move away. That way you can still maintain a relationship together while still visiting your parents or family from time to time. Even if you have to visit them separately you will be far enough removed to maintain a loving relationship without the people in your family's life being none the wiser. You won't be around enough for your father to feel the need to explain who you are to the people in his life. That way they won't ever realize that the guy their daughter is dating is actually her brother."

We both sat there speechless staring at Dr. Buckley

"It's really the only way. The only thing that I could recommend is to get your father to come in and the three of you can hash out your feelings and I can be the mediator."

"That's never going to happen." I stated plainly.

"Well then…"

She stared at me expectantly. "I can't move," I whispered. The whole time I was thinking how I could possibly walk away from the great job I had, never mind my best friend Donna or my sister and other relatives. I loved my parents but I wasn't sure how big of a role they fit in my life any longer. But the rest, I would surely miss terribly.

"Why can't you?"

I was shocked to find the question came from Jeff. "I have a great job here Jeff, the first great one I've ever had."

"You're an administrative assistant Carrie, you could do that any-where."

"So you're okay with moving? What about the company you run?"

"Well we have lots of different divisions." He looked to Dr. Buck-ley, "I'm assuming when you suggest we move somewhere that it's far away?"

My mouth hung open as I saw her nod. "The farther the better; I would suggest out of the country."

"What? Jeff you can't possibly be serious?"

"Maybe. I would have to discuss it with my right hand man but we do have a division in Paris after all. You worked there with me yourself. I could take you on as my assistant once again. Let's be honest you wouldn't even have to work, we could get married. They are so much more secretive over there about situations such as ours. It is much less frowned upon over there. It would actually be perfect. You could stay home and follow your own dreams in-stead of mine."

"But what about my friends…and my sister?"

"Come on Carrie. I have a lot of money. You could travel home any time you wanted to and visit them. Or fly them in, that really doesn't matter."

"Marvelous. Spend a few years in France Carrie and Jeff and see if your parents don't see your situation differently after that."

I was still in shock. One minute we were discussing our relationship and the next we were formulating a plot to get married and move to Paris. It was almost too much for my brain to process.

"Is this really what we want? To change our entire life? I won't know anyone in Paris."

"I think it is what we want sweetie. To get married and to have a life together without all the judgement. Paris is gorgeous and it would be your playground. Plus my father has been living there for the past few years so we would know someone. You will meet new friends. I have a lot of connections in Paris. It really does make sense for us right now. It doesn't have to be forever. If we hate it then we come back, it's pretty simple."

I looked to Dr. Buckley, "Is this really going to work?"

She smiled warmly for the first time since we had been there. "Carrie, France doesn't mind the idea of close relations so to speak. You and Jeff don't share the same last names and France does not require a couple to get blood tests done before they are married. So it's the perfect place to start over. No one would really know that you were siblings. In the meantime it would give your parents the break they need to fully realize what they are missing by not having you in their lives regularly. To be honest though, they may never realize it but at least you will have a relationship that you want without feeling pressured."

Looking at Jeff, I took a deep breath. "Okay let's do this."

Chapter Seventeen

Jeff

Driving home from the counselling session Carrie still hadn't spoken a word to me. I knew she was pretty freaked out by the session and I had to wonder if it had been the best thing for us. I couldn't deny the brilliance of Dr. Buckley's advice though, it made perfect sense. Moving away would change everything for us; allow us the freedom we needed to be ourselves, to grow in our relationship. I looked at her as she glanced out the window and I was starting to become afraid that she had grown mute. I knew that she didn't want to move away but I was actually exhilarated by the idea of a fresh start. To start over from scratch was very appealing indeed. The idea of moving to a new country and running a new division got my creative juices flowing anew once again. I thought it was important to revamp yourself every now and again to keep a good challenge going, to keep you fresh. Paris was a very diverse area to live in as well as the fact that it was also very freeing. There were not the same expectations as there were in North America and we could do more in our relationship there than we ever could living at home. No one would care that I had married my step-sister; there were bigger scandals than that going on in that country. There was also the benefit that I would also be able to maintain a relationship with my biological father without him being weirded out by my new wife. It was very important to me to have him in my life. I knew that Carrie understood that, but I also knew that she didn't have the same desire as I did to stay in contact with her father. If she lost him forever she wouldn't blink an eye. I however just found him and I desired to know my real father without problems. By having us out of the country I could travel back and forth to see them, fly them into Paris without there being scandalous talk in my father's neighborhood.

I watched her for a moment. "Are you okay Carrie? You haven't spoken one word to me since we left. Are you mad at me?"

She glanced my way and smiled. "No, of course not. I'm just confused and a little scared." She shrugged.

Her response puzzled me. "There's no reason to be scared. We have all the money in the world so we have no worries in that respect. The sky is the limit for you and you can choose to work for me or start something up for yourself. You have the freedom to do whatever you would like. How many people get that chance in life? Be reasonable Carrie, you have everything you could ever ask for."

She nodded but was still frowning. "I know. I'm very lucky. I'm sorry. It's just not what I expected. That's all. I just wished that there was another way."

I looked out the windshield. "Right now there isn't. We need to try this first."

"You don't even know if they will want you to go to Paris. What if the company wants you to stay here? Then what are we going to do?"

"Oh believe me darling, that is the least of my worries. They need someone like me in Paris. I could kill it there; bring a whole new brand to that division."

"You know they aren't going to come to the wedding right?" She glanced out the side window again. I couldn't help but wonder if she was trying to find any excuse possible to not go. We needed to go to Paris; I truly believed that it was the best possible solution for us. We had to at least try and see if it would be the miracle that we were looking for.

"Jeff?"

I knew she was referring to our father and her mother going to our wedding. It was unfortunate that we wouldn't have our parents at the wedding but how could we expect any different? There was no doubt in my mind that they would not come but we had to move forward with the plan anyways; it was the best that we could do at that point and who knows, maybe in the future things would change. Maybe once they realized we were serious and not backing out they would decide to just be a part of our lives. It was the most that we could ask for at that point. In the meantime it would be Paris.

"Yeah, I know they won't. As long as you are there however nothing else matters. We will get through this together just like we planned. We got back together for a reason didn't we?"

She finally turned to me and smiled. "Yes, I know. I just didn't expect it to come to this I guess. But I do love you and whatever you think is best, I will go along with."

"You look absolutely stunning by the way; you always do; if that makes you feel any better." I joked, trying to keep the smile on her face. I just wanted her to be happy. If I could accomplish that then maybe I could let go of what my father thought about our relationship. It wouldn't be easy but I had to focus on my future with my soon-to-be wife.

"Well it certainly can't hurt." She grasped my hand in hers and squeezed it.

"That's what I like to hear."

"Maybe we should get drunk." She said.

I laughed, "I'm not sure that's going to help our situation. It fact it probably won't help."

"Why?"

"You getting drunk is not going to help. In fact it will probably only make you feel worse. We both have to get up early tomorrow for work. It's going to be okay Carrie I promise you."

She frowned, "I think you need to take me to your place."

I looked into her eyes, held her gaze, not wavering. "Are you sure? We don't have to do anything tonight."

"Yes, I need to forget everything for now. Or at least a few hours. My head is clogged and you need to clear it for me."

I nodded and I picked up the pace heading towards my home instead of dropping her off at her own. We arrived at my home and I left the car out front to be parked. She looked lost as she got out of the car. I took her hand and led her inside.

I wasn't sure why she wanted to forget everything especially since it was about to be our whole life. But I would allow her an evening to forget the plan. We would have to talk about things again tomorrow however we had plenty of plans to make and they would not wait. I would have to discuss things with the company and make a plan to move. It would be a lot of work, even after I got to Paris but I felt that in the end it would be worth it.

She walked around my home looking rattled and I wondered if I should make her a drink to help her mind settle. No, I thought, I could settle her mind myself with very little effort. It was my gift. She was my gift too. I came up behind her, putting my mouth on her shoulder. Her skin was salty to the taste and I lingered there. She turned around to face me and kissed me full on the mouth. Her mouth was hot against mine and I suddenly felt warm all over, the heat travelling instantly to my pants. Our tongues molded together with heat building up between us; it was always that way with Carrie. She could turn me on so easily. She moaned aching in every part of her body for me; I could feel it as she pressed up against me. I kissed her mouth, her chin and lingered on her neck nipping my way down. I loved the taste of her skin and it was causing me to have an ache of my own. I was throbbing for her and I could not wait to bury myself inside of her. Feeling the soft folds of her around my cock would be the best feeling in the world.

"Please, I need you now. Please don't make me wait." She whimpered. The sound of her voice and the fact that she was begging for my cock made it that much harder in my pants. I needed to release it and push inside her.

I picked her up and carried her to the master bedroom.

"I miss you Jeff, even though we are together all the time. I need you badly."

"I know darling, I missed you too. I always do."

She looked around the room after I brought her in and set her down. "It looks like you have something rough in store for me." She looked up at me surprised.

"Well I think you've been a bad girl darling, keeping me away from your beautiful pussy for so long. I can't stop thinking about you when I'm in the office and you are no longer there for me to bend you over."

"Bad? Oh really?" She asked with a glint in her eye.

"Yes and you need to be punished. A good...hard punishing should make you see that you belong in Paris." I said with a grin on my face.

"You wouldn't believe how wet I'm getting just from you talking that way to me." She began to undress, sliding the straps of her lace dress off her shoulders and letting it fall to the floor. She was completely nude underneath the dress and she smiled as I looked her over. She looked insanely gorgeous and I couldn't wait to have her. How had I got so lucky to find her? She blew my mind. I undressed showing her a completely rock hard cock ready to punish her just the way I wanted, it's all I could think about.

I led her to the bed and bent her over. Her ass looked gloriously round before me and I bent down to kiss it. God, she was so hot. She knew I was going to take her from behind and give it to her hard. I picked up a paddle and slapped her bottom with it. She gasped and I swore I could make her cum just like that.

"You're mine Carrie, all mine."

She moaned.

"Say it. Tell me your mine Carrie."

She giggled, "I'm yours Jeff. I'm all yours baby. Take me."

I paddled her ass again and drove my cock into her. She cried out and I plunged in deeper and deeper every time. She was moaning so loudly that I thought I would lose my mind. It was the best sound in the world. I could listen to her moan all day long she was just that hot.

I pushed in a butt plug while I fucked her. She was getting hit in various nerves while I fucked her quite perfectly. It was obvious she didn't know how much she could take and she came all over my cock. I flipped her over putting my hands around her throat, her voice caught just as I plunged my cock into her. Her eyes fluttered as she got completely foggy and lightheaded, it looked like she might pass out. I released her throat, pumping inside her hard and fast. Carrie came so hard her whole body rocked against me. I fucked her with the butt plug while tantalizing her pussy with my hard cock.

"Oh Jeff, you feel so good, I can't stand it."

"Oh baby, you are perfect. Every single part of you. You are so wet I need to be inside you all the time."

She came again; her face showed me all I needed to know about how she felt. She was completely taken by me, I didn't know if I could ever leave her side again. She had stayed with me despite the madness. I would do anything for her because of that.

I filled her full of cum and collapsed on top of her. She kissed the top of my head trying to catch her breath. She smelled incredible and it almost caused me to grown hard again.

We lay there for an hour, not speaking just holding each other tight. She wasn't sure what was going to happen next, I knew that much. I didn't know what was right and what was wrong anymore. All my decisions had still led to this moment there with Carrie. This moment where I knew we could never go back. I would marry her and take her life to Paris; there would be no going back from that. We would need to build a life together and band together forever.

It had always been Carrie; he had stood by her no matter what her decisions were, how could I not? I think I fell in love with her the moment I walked into that diner that day. She had been so fresh and innocent and my god I had no idea that she was my step-sister.

116

I knew she couldn't live like that anymore always wondering if I would be by her side. I needed to commit to her and prove to her I would be there. I knew I had put my fair effort into the relationship and shouldn't feel any guilt about being with her. But I did however because I loved her and I knew deep down she loved me and that my worst fears would come true if I couldn't give her the life I promised.

We were going to start living the life we wanted, the life she should have had from the beginning. I would grab a hold of Carrie and never let her go. It was her turn to shine and be loved in the way in which she deserved. I owed her that much at least.

"I need to go Jeff." She whispered against my chest.

"Where?"

"Home. I need to think about all this, and I need to do it alone."

"Let me get dressed and I will come with you."

She laughed, "You know that's not going to happen. I said I need some time alone to think."

"I would stand beside you up against any adversary. Let's do this together."

She looked into my eyes and smiled. "I know you would, but this is something I need to do on my own, for me. I want to talk things over with Donna too; it's all a pretty big deal to me."

"I'm here if you need me, I won't leave this room until I hear from you."

She kissed me on the mouth, jumping out of bed to get dressed. She said good bye and headed for the door.

Chapter Eighteen

Carrie

Sitting across the table from Donna, we snacked on cheese and crackers with tea and discussed my latest endeavor. I needed my friend to help me make a decision. To help me see things the way that Jeff did and to tell me that everything was going to be alright.

"So let me get this straight?"

I took a sip my tea and waited for what I assumed would be an attack since Donna was already beginning things off with a dash of sarcasm.

"You have a millionaire boyfriend who wants to whisk you off to Paris and marry your ass. And you get to live happily ever after in the City of Love and you don't know what you want to do? Come on Carrie, is this a real question? Do you really not know what to do?"

I laughed; Donna always knew how to put things in perspective for me. "Well when you say it like that, I really do sound stupid. But I would be leaving everything behind. Wouldn't you miss me?"

Donna stuck her tongue out. "You know I would, how can you even ask that? But that's hardly the point Carrie. Come on, I'm not going anywhere, I'm not dying. You can come and see me any time that you want. But this is a chance of a lifetime; you don't want to miss out on this. I would kill for an opportunity like that. What's really the problem?"

Tears suddenly welled up in my eyes. "God, I don't know. I'm not sure what's wrong with me."

"It's a lot to take in Carrie, I'm sure. It's a huge change, a big move but look at all the good things about it. What an exciting adventure awaits you. Imagine being able to wake up in Paris."

"I know. It's just so scary."

"Well you wanted to get out from under the rule of your parents and now you will be. That's all that matters."

"Yes, I know. You're right."

"So stop mopping around and grab Jeff by the horns and live happily ever after. Just watch out for the other women."

I frowned, "Other women, what do you mean?"

"Well France may be forgiving when it comes to siblings shaking up but they are also very forgiving when it comes to mistresses. It's actually pretty common for married men to have a woman on the side."

"You can't be serious. We don't live in the 20's anymore."

"I'm dead serious. It's always been that way. It didn't just happen in the 20's."

Shocked, I tried to picture Jeff taking up with a mistress. The good thing about that thought was that I couldn't believe for a minute that he would do anything like that.

"There's no way that Jeff would do something like that."

She laughed, "Well of course he wouldn't. I'm just warning you is all."

"Well let's just forget the whole thing, because I don't like thinking about that at all."

We hugged tightly and I suddenly felt much better about everything. I refused to think about Jeff and France and....mistresses.

I was waiting for Jeff at his home when he arrived home that evening. He came through the front door with a huge smile on his face and a bottle of champagne.

"Thank you for meeting me here Carrie, I have some great news for us."

I smiled warmly but my stomach fluttered nervously. I didn't know what to say or do. I couldn't imagine what he could have to celebrate but I could use the drink.

"I was surprised when you asked me over. Did you have a good day at the office? A promotion maybe?"

He chuckled. "Come now Carrie, you know very well I have no intention of taking a promotion at the office here. I have better plans for us."

I watched as he went about getting a couple of flutes. He poured us some champagne and brought them over. Handing me one he slipped in beside me on the couch. "What are we celebrating?"

"Well the company it turns out is doing quite well in Paris. I spoke with the board about moving there and they thought it was a brilliant idea. They want to move my division there and they want to set things up immediately."

"You're kidding me? Already? But it's so fast. How did this all happen?"

"Because it makes sense for the company, that's why. I told you that already, it makes sense for me to be there and get the company to a new level in Paris; just like I did here. It's going to be amazing. I want you to pack right away because we are leaving tomorrow morning."

"What? What about my job? I can't just leave without giving them notice, some time to find a replacement for me."

"Carrie, I've already taken care of it. I've spoken to your boss; I got you the job you have, remember? It's no big deal. They understand."

Anger flared up inside of me. "Jeff, you had no right to do that. You can't just commandeer my life and not allow me to have an opinion of my own. I'm not ready this is all happening too fast."

He frowned as he watched me. "Please Carrie we have to do this and unfortunately the office in Paris has to be set up immediately. I can't just wait until you feel up to going. If you want this we have to do it now."

I downed the full glass of champagne and poured another. Jeff watched me with what appeared to be concern in his eyes. "Please Carrie. We need this."

I nodded although I didn't want to go. It was too soon. I wasn't ready and I could barely catch my breath. I would do whatever he wanted however, if it made him happy. We would make it work no matter what happened.

He leaned over and kissed me. "Please don't worry Carrie; everything is going to be okay. I promise you. You just have to trust me."

"I do trust you."

"We both love Paris; remember how much fun we had there? The fashion, the clothes you bought the glamourous lifestyle? It could all be worth it."

"I know. It does sound very exciting. I can't wait, really."

His mouth was on mine again and we kissed for a long time. I grabbed him by the back of the neck and pulled him in to me. We locked lips and it was like they lit on fire. God, he was such a good kisser. I really couldn't get enough of his mouth on mine. I was completely addicted to him, that much I could not deny. I had to forget about the whole whirlwind that was the Paris plan. I needed to do this in order to make things work with Jeff.

We kissed our tongues teasing one another as I began taking off his jacket and pulling at his tie. I sucked on his tongue gently and he ripped at my clothes pawing at my breasts. I knew I was driving him wild and I sort of liked it. Our hands were all over each other as I unbuttoned his shirt and tore it off. He unzipped my dressed and I stepped out of it revealing my sexy underwear. I was already buzzing on champagne and I couldn't wait to have the man of my dreams inside of me. He was all I ever thought about, so why was I making the move to Paris so difficult for us. I was being stupid. I wanted him and this was the best way to have him.

"Wow, you look incredible. I want you Carrie. I want you on my cock. Suck it really hard baby."

I loved when he talked that way to me. I would suck him really good. His cock made me so horny and I wanted it in my mouth. I moaned as I fumbled with his belt buckle and slid the zipper down on his pants. They dropped to his ankles and I did the same to his underwear. He stepped out of them easily and there before me was a nice thick cock. He was huge and his cock stood out in great length causing me to gasp when I saw it. It didn't matter how many times I saw it, it just made me warm just looking at it. He was hot and his cock looked too good to be true. I wanted him in my mouth and then in my pussy. No wonder the guy chose to fuck me every chance he got, it was perfect and yet I almost feared his size. He quickly released me of my undergarments and I saw his eyes flicker towards my pussy. He wanted me I could tell and I was about to see what kind of fuck he was going to give me this time.

I bent down before him and took him into my mouth; I ached for him. This would be a true test of my gag reflex and I almost giggled at the thought of it. I sucked on his hard cock while I played with his balls. He was groaning above me his hands in my hair. I loved hearing him moan when I was pleasing him so. It brought me more pleasure than my own orgasm. He moaned my name and I just sucked harder. His noises were making me wet and I couldn't wait to have him inside of me. My tongue twirled around the tip of his cock and all I could think about at that moment was pleasing him as best I could. It was the most important thing to me. My tongue rubbed up against his shaft as I sucked on his cock. I could tell by the way he was tugging on my hair that he was horny and about to come undone. I would not allow him to cum quite yet however; I wanted him to come inside me that is all.

He pulled me up from him and picked me up in his arms. He carried me over to the bedroom and onto his bed where he laid me down. Jeff looked down at me with a heat in his eyes I had never seen before. That was what I loved about him, he was always surprising me. Every time we were together it felt different and I couldn't imagine that we would ever get bored of one another in the bedroom. I smiled at him as he then climbed on top of me and spread my legs. I was so ready for him. He admired my pussy as if he couldn't wait to lick me. I was already wet; the experience for me was highly erotic and it was actually quite easy to forget that we were off to Paris in the morning. Everything else was drowned out by the look that was in Jeff's eyes.

Jeff bent down and his mouth was on my pussy immediately. I closed my eyes, enjoying every moment of his tongue as it lapped at me over and over again. He was so good at it. I moaned as he tasted my most intimate area and his eyes met mine. My eyes burned as I watched his mouth on my pussy. He was so incredibly hot that I melted right into his mouth. He's licking and sucking and it made me dizzy. God, I couldn't imagine I was going to cum right into his mouth. I had never had such passionate sex before. He was so good at licking my pussy that I almost didn't want him to stop. He definitely knew what he was doing when it came to oral sex. He began to suck on my clit while he pushed two fingers inside me. I moaned loudly as the sensations felt so incredible. Waves of pleasure coursed through me and I moaned again as I came against his fingers. It was almost too much to take all at once. He fucked me so good that he blew my mind every single time. He pumped his fingers inside me harder as he tickled my pussy with his tongue. He was finger fucking me really good and I felt myself going a little bit mad from all the pleasure, it was almost too much to take and yet I was not going to have him stop. Not for a moment. He took his fingers out and lay down on the couch pulling me up with him.

"Wow Jeff, that was so good. I want more baby please."

"Not so fast my love. Suck my cock Carrie. Suck the cum right out of me. Let's 69 so I get the best of both worlds."

I grinned up at him thinking about his cock once again. I knew what was next and I positioned myself on top of him so that my pussy was right in his face. I took his huge cock into my mouth once again as his tongue entered the opening of my pussy. He tickled the lips of my opening and my eyelids fluttered shut. I groaned with his cock in my mouth. I sucked on him hard just as he requested. It was extremely hard to concentrate on what I was doing when his mouth was sucking on my clit. I thought I might pass out at some point. All I wanted was to get fucked and I could barely contain my excitement. "I'm going to cum Baby."

Jeff came in my mouth before and I began sucking him much slower this time. I literally sucked the rest of the cum out of him until there was nothing left. The saltiness of him took over my taste buds and I licked the tip of his cock when I was finished.

"Don't think you are done there sexy boy. I want your cock inside me. So get ready to go again."

He smiled, "Anything for you my love." I continued to rub his cock until he grew hard once again. "God, baby you are so sexy I can't believe I get to fuck you any time I want to."

I kissed him hard on the mouth. Jeff smiled and when I pulled away from him he whispered for me to relax and follow his lead. I pushed him back on the bed feeling lustful all over again. His eyes lit up and I enjoyed the fact that he liked my aggressive side. My mouth enveloped his cock and I sucked on him to get him back as hard as he was. As I bounced on his cock I let my tongue slide around his cock causing him to groan loudly. I enjoyed bringing him pleasure and I sucked on him hard until he started calling out my name. My tongue swirled around the tip of his shaft slowly as my fingers played with his balls. I wasn't able to deep throat him very well, but I did the best I could, feeling his cock hit the back of my throat repeatedly. He pulled his cock from my mouth and I smiled, knowing what was coming next.

Jeff climbed on top of me and pushed his fingers inside my pussy roughly claiming it as his own. He pumped inside me hard and fast, building an orgasm inside me that I knew was going to be big. Just before I thought I might cum he put his head in between my legs and sucked on my clit hard. I moaned deeply coming into his mouth at the same time.

"Baby please I need you to fuck me. I'm throbbing for you."

He continued to lick my pussy, licking up every drop of my cum. I moaned loudly as he licked around my opening and stuck his tongue inside. He went back to finger fucking me until I exploded once more. He moved above me and I smiled up at him. I was in the missionary position and he pushed in close to me so that my pussy was slammed up against him and he positioned my legs so that they were in a V-position on either side of him. The position allowed him to be very close to me so that he could bend down and kiss me fully on the lips. He plunged his large cock inside me and I cried out as he filled me up. His size was incredible and I was delirious with the size of him. Jeff fucked me slowly allowing me to adjust to his size. Even being fucked slowly by his cock was maddening. He rubbed up against every nerve inside me and nuzzled against my G-spot. I thought for sure I was going to cum again and he had barely fucked me. I moaned loudly with every thrust he pushed inside me and I wasn't sure if I could stand any more. My orgasm was slowly building again and Jeff moved to change our position. He slid out of me and I missed the feeling of fullness that he had given me.

He flipped me over roughly so that I was lying on my stomach. I giggled when he did so. It excited me when we tried new positions it made our sex life that much more exciting. It was always something different. The position Jeff chose was very similar to doggy style except I was to lay flat with just a slight raise in my hips. I cried out once again as he entered me. It was a tight fit and the position made Jeff feel even larger inside of me if that was actually possible. It was a deep fuck and I knew I would not be able to hold off my orgasm if he decided to switch positions again. I moaned with every thrust feeling very wantonly beneath him. He felt incredible and between the size of him and his skilled positioning, I didn't think I had ever been fucked as good before. The waves of pleasure coursing through my body build up to an insane feeling and I cried out Jeff's name as an orgasm shook me all over. He smacked my ass as he slipped out of me causing me to gasp in surprise.

"You're driving me crazy Jeff."

He grinned at me as he switched positions again. This one he called the G-Whiz and it was meant to specifically target the G-spot. It was similar to the first position except Jeff rested my legs on his shoulders. With my legs up so high it allowed him to get

126

nice and deep and in the perfect spot to hit my G-spot over and over again. He entered me once again causing a dizziness to come over me. I had never felt so good and I didn't want that feeling to end. I had an orgasm repeatedly that night, which was something that had never happened to me before. I wanted more. I couldn't get enough of him and I was receiving endless waves of pleasure.

He fucked me hard in that position and I had a repeat orgasm while he did it. I was consumed with lust. Not only was Jeff really deep but he was plunging inside me mercilessly and I ached all over with need. If it was possible for a man to make you horny and satisfy you all at once than that was the feeling that he instilled in me. I wanted and needed him at the same time I was receiving the pleasure I needed from him. It was a crazy sensation and I was becoming addicted to the feeling.

"Oh god Carrie, oh baby I'm going to cum."

He pulled out then and squeezed his cock. Cum sprayed out all over my chest in a milky stream. Another first for me, he had never come on me before. I lay there beneath him spent. My chest was heaving and I could barely even move. I knew for sure I would be sore the next day but it was a soreness I would revel in and love every minute of it. I had just been fucked properly and I was in the afterglow. I was breathing heavily and I was not even sure if I was still on the same planet but one thing was for sure, I was grinning like an idiot.

Jeff leaned down towards me and kissed me softly on the lips. I kissed him back and enjoyed the soft feeling of his lips against mine. I could kiss that guy all day long; he was just that good at it. He was the best kisser I had ever known in my young life. There was just something about being kissed by Jeff that made you just want to fuck him mercilessly.

"Not bad baby. You are such a good fuck," he's rubbing my inner thigh as he whispered in my ear; "How do you feel?"

"I feel incredible. How could I not? You put quite the effort in with all those positions."

"I just wanted to make you feel better, you have been so sad lately and I don't like it."

I couldn't even deny him his touching as it felt just as incredible as the fuck I just had. I liked the fact that his hands were still in between my legs massaging my inner thighs. I was still in awe of how good he was with his cock. He thought I was a good fuck but really it was all him. His size, his movements and the fact that he knew when to fuck me slowly and went to be a little rough.

And tomorrow we would be off to Paris to start a new life together. It was certainly enough to blow your mind.

He climbed off of me but not before kissing me one last time on the lips. "How about some more champagne?"

I smiled, "I would love some, thank you."

And with that we spent our last night in the United States.

Chapter Nineteen
Carrie

The wedding is tomorrow, holy shit, I thought. I had been rushing around all day trying to get the last minute details down. To be truthful I was exhausted. I was looking forward to a peaceful night at home relaxing before I married the man of my dreams in the morning. It had all happened faster than I thought even though we didn't get married as soon as we arrived in Paris. In fact it had been a rather stressful few months when we first arrived. I had barely seen Jeff the whole time because he was setting up his office in the new building. He had been working 16 hour days and when he did manage to get home he was too exhausted. We hadn't made love in forever and I was starting to ache for him in way that I couldn't full describe. I was lonely and we had not even been married yet. I loved him dearly but I didn't want to be in a marriage where I never saw my husband. Jeff assured me however that things would slow down soon and he would have more time to spend with me.

We had decided that I would stay at home and try to figure out a career of my own, something that I could be passionate about. I had yet to figure that out however I was still adjusting to the Paris life. I regretted not going to work for Jeff because then I would have been part of his day, part of the chaos that kept him from home. I would be able to surprise him with afternoon delights any time I wanted to. Instead I was stuck at home while he worked all hours of the day and night. He assured me however that things would be different once we got married and settled in. His assistant was a thin woman with jet black hair that fell halfway down her back. Her body reminded me of the counsellor we had in the States. The body that Jeff had admired while we sat in the office discussing our future with Dr. Buckley. I tried not to let it bother me that his new assistant was exotic and sexy. My mind just kept wandering to what Donna had said to me about married men taking lovers in Paris. It didn't help that we weren't having the crazy sex that we used to have. Men needed to have sex didn't they? How was Jeff coping if he was not having sex with me? No, I refused to believe he was having sex with anyone else. It just wasn't possible. We had worked so hard to be together he wouldn't betray me like that. It was just inconceivable.

Donna and a few other friends flew in to be part of the wedding. My parents wouldn't be there of course but Jeff's father would be attending so I guess we would have some family there. The bridal party wanted to take me out for dinner and hang out all evening but it wasn't how I wanted to spend my last night as an unmarried woman. I didn't want to be hungover and tired on my wedding day. I just wanted to stay home and relax and let things be natural. I was going to open a bottle of wine and relish my night alone. Tomorrow I would be a married woman and could start my new life with my guy. It was all finally starting to fall into place.

Jeff had wanted to get married right away, he had even suggested eloping. I refused however which was why we found ourselves in Paris for a few months before we tied the knot. I planned on only getting married once in my life so I wanted the wedding of my dreams. I would not settle for less just because Jeff wanted to rush into things. I had announced to my father we were getting married, however he was so angry on the phone he sounded like he wanted to murder me so the idea of my parents coming to the wedding was a big no. After meeting with a wedding planner we had a date set for a month and a half later after arriving in Paris. Invites and announcements were sent out immediately. Most of his friends had never met me before so they had no idea that I was really his sister. We had originally wanted to keep things small but things had quickly gotten out of hand when it came to the invites.

The planning went flawlessly and I didn't feel at all like I had been a usual Bridezilla. Maybe happiness does that to a person because that was how I felt truly happy.

When I finally arrived at our studio apartment after a long day of shopping I was tired and so looking forward to that bottle of wine.

At least everything was in order as it should be. I was so excited for the morning to come. The wedding would be wonderfully perfect and we would be flying out for our honeymoon immediately afterwards. I couldn't wait to experience that with Jeff, it would be yet another one of our adventures.

I opened the door to our place, set my bags down and finally sighed with relief. Everything was finished I just had to wait until morning to get married.

I was uncorking the bottle of wine when there was a knock on the door. Puzzled I couldn't imagine who would be showing up now, everyone knew I was getting married the next day so they would just assume I didn't want company. Jeff had not arrived home from the office yet. I couldn't believe he was still working on the night before our wedding, but there was nothing I could seem to do to talk him out of it.

I set the bottle down, and poured a tall glass before going to answer the door. When the door swung open the glass of wine fell from my hand and smashed on the floor.

"What the hell are you doing here?"

Jeff's assistant stood there, her long black hair flowing around her shoulders. There was just something about the look on her face that angered me to no end. I didn't want her there one the eve of my wedding and I wasn't sure why it bothered me so much. She had no right to be there.

A slight smile crossed her face and it made me want to scream. I glanced down at the broken glass at my feet and I suddenly knew that something was very wrong.

"We need to talk."

So we did.

Chapter Twenty

Carrie

I stood there feeling indignant about the fact that Cassandra, Jeff's assistant was standing in my doorway on the night before my wedding. She was quite truly the last person that I had expected to see. I had thought maybe Donna would have shown up and dragged me out of the house but she was probably out enjoying Paris, knowing that I wanted to be alone and not hungover for my wedding. The gall of this woman though to think that she could come there and talk to me.

The shocking part of it all was that I was sure that I knew why she was there. The woman had done nothing to me that I knew of yet the sight of her caused so much anger to build up inside of me. Was it justified? Well that depended on what she was doing at my home. Sometimes women just know things. They know why their husband works so late even though they have a hard time accepting the truth. They just swallow one excuse after another, hoping that it's all true. Jeff was working hard; he had to set up a whole new division in Paris. It was the whole reason why they had moved there to begin with. That much at least had been true. But the long exhausting hours, the fact that sometimes he didn't come how at all, just slept on his office couch because he worked too late. But had he really been working that late? Or did he stay out somewhere else.

The fact that Cassandra was at my door looking so smug sent alarms ringing off in my head. She was going to tell me wasn't she? On the eve of my wedding I was about to get some news that I wasn't sure that I could live with. Jeff and I had worked so hard to be together, we had literally moved out of the country to try and make things work. Had he really cheated on me within a month of being there? It was a little hard to comprehend. Why would he do such a thing? We were supposed to be a team, to work together and try as hard as we could to stay together. Would he really do something so thoughtless and cruel after everything we had been through together?

"Cassandra, is it? What are you doing here at this hour? I have quite a long day ahead of me as you well know."

"As I said Carrie, we need to talk."

"I can't imagine about what? Does Jeff know you are here?"

"No, he doesn't and I would like to keep it that way."

I raised my eyebrows. It was getting worse the more she spoke. I knew I wasn't going to like this conversation. I smirked. "Well I can't make any promises but we'll see."

Cassandra narrowed her eyes at me. "Do you mind if I come in or should we have this conversation out in the hallway."

I moved aside and motioned for her to come inside my home. I had a bad feeling about the whole thing. Deep down I knew I had a reason why I didn't want her in my own, near my things, especially my husband to be. She looked at me like a puma about to pounce on its prey. I stood my ground however and my gaze never wavered from hers.

"What do you want Cassandra?"

"I want you to cancel the wedding."

I stared at her hoping that she was going to burst out laughing and admit that it was all just a joke. It had to be right? What woman in their right mind would come to someone's home with such a request? It was disgusting to say the least.

"Excuse me? What is wrong with you Cassandra? Why would I even consider doing such a thing? I love Jeff very much and I have every intention of marrying him."

"Jeff is mine. He has been since he got here. It actually didn't take a whole lot of effort to get him into my bed. I want him for myself. So that leaves you out, I want to marry Jeff."

My head was reeling from what she had told me. I couldn't even believe my ears. Were all Paris women so forward and confident? She had no qualms about coming into my home and nonchalantly telling me to hand over my fiancé. The woman had to be a mad-woman. Who does such a thing on the night before a wedding? Ahh, but wasn't that how they did things in the movies? Except then they liked to leave it until the couple was at the alter before someone would step up and profess their love for the bride or groom. It didn't feel any more real to me than if I was in a movie. I couldn't believe what was happening. Jeff loved me, I knew that. How could he be sleeping with this woman, and for the entire time we had been in Paris? He sure hadn't wasted any time. I felt ill thinking about them together and knowing full well it was all true. I didn't even need to ask him. Like I said, women just know. The whole office was probably talking about it. I was never there so how would I know? What I did know was that Jeff and I hadn't slept together in a long time. He had been just too busy and too tired when he returned home to me. But apparently he had been taking his stress out on the puma that now resided in my living room. I felt a rage seething inside of me and I wanted nothing more than to rip the woman apart.

"How dare you come into my home with this?"

"I told you why. I want Jeff for myself."

"What makes you think that I believe a word you say. You think I would call off my wedding without even talking to my husband about it first?"

"He's not your husband yet. Like I said I would rather you not. He doesn't know I am here; he didn't want you to know. He likes his secrets."

I knew that was true more than anyone. No one knew that we were siblings. It was the whole reason we had run away to Paris and now this? Everything was shot to hell because Jeff couldn't keep it in his pants. What would I do now? Return home with my tail be-tween my legs and have to admit to my father than I had failed? That Jeff had gone off with someone else. It was too humiliating to even comprehend.

"How do I know you aren't lying? If I can't confirm it with Jeff then how would I know? You could just be lying to get me away from him and you could move in for the kill. You're nothing but a slut Cassandra. Moving in on someone's fiancé is certainly a lowly act."

Cassandra didn't seem at all ruffled by the insult I threw her way. Like I said, the woman had a confidence that I did not possess. She just smirked at me in an all knowing way that irritated me to no end. I wanted to claw her eyes out and yet my fiancé was no better. He was the one that had allowed such a woman into our lives. Was that why he had done it? She was so confident and exuded that in a very possessive sexual way. Was that what he liked, what he craved?

"You know. Carrie you aren't a dumb girl. No one needs to work that many hours and stay in an office overnight. I think you probably had your worries long before I showed up at your door. But if it helps confirm anything for you, I know he has a birth mark in the shape of a heart on his ass. I've actually licked it."

I slapped her hard across the face and watched her head snap to the side with glee. That was going to leave a mark. One that she could parade around with at my wedding. If she thought for a moment I was just going to sit back and allow her to stop in for a visit and request my husband on a platter she was sadly mistaken. I would deal with Jeff in a manner of my own choosing and if anyone was going to go it would not be me.

Cassandra straightened herself up even though she had tears in her eyes and a red mark on her face. Confident until the end I guess.

"I guess I deserved that."

"You would guess correctly. Now maybe you should get the hell out of my home before I do worse to you."

"Do you really want to stay with someone who's going to carry on a mistress? It's Paris Carrie; things are a little different here. My god Hemingway came here and had a mistress for years while his wife knew about it. That's what you have to look forward to. I'm not going anywhere that much I can guarantee. Jeff will not let me go. So if you stay you have to knowingly be okay with your husband fucking me whenever he sees fit. I wouldn't even bother looking at your credit card bill anymore either unless you want to see all the things he buys me."

I was speechless, literally shocked into silence. I could not believe what I was hearing. I couldn't even believe that she said it as if she was just talking about items she purchased at a grocery store. She was a cold and calculated bitch and it wasn't going to be easy getting her out of my life. Was she telling the truth when she said that Jeff would not give her up? I could only hope that he wasn't in love with her. If it was sex, I could handle it. If he loved her however that was entirely different. I would not be able to live with that. Jeff was no Hemingway and I wasn't about to sit around while my husband fell in love with another woman. I wouldn't have it.

"Well aren't you pleased with yourself. Does it not bother you that you are the kind of shrewd woman you goes after things that don't belong to you. Can you not find a boyfriend of your own?"

"But Carrie, that's what I did. I do have something that is mine. If you marry him then you have to be okay with the fact that he has himself a Paris mistress. I know you Americans have a hard time with things like that but it's all very common in Paris. Do you think you can live like that?"

The conversation I had with Donna all came flooding back. She had warned me about this and I had laughed it off like it was nothing. Yet Jeff hadn't wasted any time jumping on that bandwagon. He humiliated me in the process as well. I was outraged and yet I was also out of my league. I had no idea how to handle the situation or how to get my fiancé back. Cassandra's confident ate away at me and made me wonder if I even had a shot of getting rid of her. Would I have to accept the fact that he had a mistress and just try to ignore that fact. I wasn't sure that I could. The thought sickened me.

"You have so much confidence Cassandra. I actually envy that about you. But aren't you worried about the same fate. What if I walked away and allowed you to have Jeff. What's to stop him from getting a new mistress after he made you his wife?"

Cassandra smirked. "That would never happen. I give him everything he needs Carrie. He doesn't need anyone else."

My cheeks burned with embarrassment. "I think it's time you left."

She nodded. "Don't tell him Carrie, you will regret it I promise you."

With that she left and I slammed the door behind her before bursting into tears.

Chapter Twenty-One

Jeff

Finishing the last bit of paperwork that I had at the office was turning to be more trying than ever. I was looking forward to going home to Carrie and spending the night with her before our wedding. Things were going to be very different between the two of us. Not only were we going to be married but I was hoping that at some point we could discuss some of the traditions that a lot of my business partners were partaking in Paris. There was no doubt in my mind that I loved Carrie, I did from the moment I met her. But there was also a lot of stress attached to the relationship I had with her as well as some sacrifices. It was really nice to wind down with someone who didn't have any of those associations. I knew that Carrie would not take it well if she found out I had been having an affair for the past month. I had been reluctant to start it but Cassandra wasn't the kind of girl that you said no to. She made you not want to say no to her. She was hot as hell and she fucked like it was going to be her last time. She allowed me to do whatever I wanted to her and begged for more. Being with Cassandra was an addiction. I used to feel that way about Carrie but we had developed more of a security towards each other. I couldn't live without Carrie; I knew that much which was why I had yet to tell her about Cassandra. I wasn't sure that she would accept that I wanted a mistress and allow our lives to go on like that. She may leave me and that was not something that I wanted. I needed to play my cards right and win her over to the idea first. I wasn't even going to try until she was my wife. She might just pick up and leave. All her friends were in town, all it would take was to get back on the plane with Donna and I would never see her again. I couldn't risk it. I needed to wait for the right opportunity.

There was a knock on my door and I looked up to find Cassandra standing there. She looked amazing in a tight black dress and stiletto heels. Normally I would find such an outfit inappropriate in the office but things were done very differently in Paris and fashion was a pretty big deal. I might as well get used to it. Not that I minded but it was hard to get any work done when she walked in looking the way she did. She smiled at me but there was something off about her smile; something hidden behind it.

"Hello Cassandra. I thought you were gone for the day."

"I was, there was something I had to do, but then I remembered that I might not see you for a while with the wedding and honeymoon in place. I wanted to leave my mark on you so you wouldn't forget me."

I chuckled, "How could I ever forget you Cassandra, you have certainly left your mark on me." I was growing hard just thinking about her. As she walked towards my desk and I knew I wanted to fuck her. I would probably not even see Carrie until the morning depending on whether she wanted to sleep apart before we were married or not. This might be the only pussy I got that day. Cassandra was always so hot and horny for me it was hard to pass up.

"Well then maybe you could leave your mark on me. I have no panties on and my pussy is already wet for you my love. I want your cock buried inside of me."

And just like that I was hard as a rock. I wanted her just as badly as she wanted me and I would give her my cock. Just then I noticed a mark on her cheek that looked like a bruise forming.

"Are you okay Cassandra? What happened to your face?" I stood up to take a closer look.

"Never mind that Jeff, it's nothing. Give me what I want."

She sat down on my desk and spread her legs her skirt ridding up on her thighs. I moved in between her legs and kissed her deeply on the mouth. She was warm and tasted sweet. I needed her after the day I had. I refused to think about Carrie while I was with Cassandra. It was easy to when Cassandra was massaging my cock through my pants. She slowly unbuckled my belt and undid my pants. They fell to my feet and she removed my underwear just as quickly.

I was standing between her beautiful legs and looking into her eyes. I couldn't help feeling excited with her being so close to me. I wanted to be inside her pussy. I knew she would already be wet and waiting for me. It was so easy to get Cassandra wet. "You are so sexy."

"Mmmm…and you are so hard. What a thick cock you have for me. I want to feel every inch of it."

I groaned, she knew exactly what to say to make me crazy for her. Sometimes I felt like I was so horny for her all the time. It had definitely affected the sex life I had with Carrie. But things were just so busy right now and there was a very fuckable woman right in the office with me. I just didn't need to wait until I got home to fuck. Not that I didn't want Carrie anymore because I did all the time but things were just so crazy at the office right now that it kept me away from home. We would be on our honeymoon though after the wedding and would have time to reconnect once again. Until then however there was Cassandra. And Cassandra wanted me to put my mark on her.

I started to rub her thighs with my hands. I held her there with a firm grip.

"Don't stop there Jeff."

I didn't, I knew what she wanted. I kept rubbing my hands up and down her milky white thighs. She had the skin of a vampire and it turned me on. "I wish that you were all mine Jeff."

"Yes, I know," I murmured underneath her lips. I slid my tongue into her mouth where hers met mine.

"Do you really have to go through with this?"

I stopped and stared at her. "Of course I do. I love Carrie. It would be different if she left me but I don't want to leave her Cassandra. I'm sorry but you knew that before we got involved."

"I know. I want you Jeff. I just don't see why you want her. She's so plain and I could give you everything that you wanted."

I stared at her then and wondered if she was going to end up being more trouble than she was worth. We had such a strong connection however I didn't want to have to give up my milky white Cassandra. I just hoped she wasn't one of those ticking time bombs that exposed me to my wife before I had the chance to talk to her about it.

"Don't do anything stupid Cassandra. That would not make me very happy."

Something flickered across her eyes that worried me slightly. I looked again at the bruise on her face and wondered where it came from.

"Let's not talk any longer, I don't want to. I just want you to make me feel fantastic. Can you do that my love?"

She took my cock in her hand and rubbed it. My eyes fluttered closed as I totally forgot about what we had been discussing. My cock felt good in her hands. She knew just how to touch me to make me forget the world around me. I had spent many nights at the office with her forgetting that anything or anyone else existed but us. She was dangerously good at that.

I sat down in my chair and started to kiss her leg, from the knee up to her thigh. Goosebumps popped up on her skin despite the heat of the office.

She knew exactly what was going to happen, and she sat there watching me to see what I would do next. She had a gorgeous smile on her face and I planned on making her feel very good indeed. My mouth moved up her leg to her bikini line, and then I kissed the top of her pussy. She moaned softly above me. I was so grateful that she didn't wear any panties; I could smell the muskiness of her and the heat that surrounded her pussy. Her smell turned me on that much more. I couldn't wait to taste her too.

I started to lick her slowly, my tongue moving in circles. She arched her head back and moaned deeply. No one else was in the office so the little minx could make all the noise that she wanted to.

"Your mouth feels so good baby."

142

I was licking up and down her pussy and then sucking on her clit. I pulled her butt closer to the edge of the desk, and ran my tongue over her hard clit, slowly at first then faster. She grabbed my hair with both hands, grinding into my face. It was the hottest thing in the world and it made me want to fuck her that much more. That was Cassandra though, she was horny and aggressive and she always got what she wanted. Her back arched and I could feel that she was coming close to the edge of an orgasm. I slipped two fingers inside of her and an orgasm exploded through her entire body. God, the pleasure she gave me with such little effort. Watching her orgasm was a sight to be seen for sure. I loved watching her cum; it was one of the sexiest experiences of my life. She brought me pleasure in so many different ways, watching her cum was just one of them. I knew I shouldn't want her and yet whenever she was near I wanted nothing more than to have her on my cock. She had a great deal of power over me. Out chemistry together was off the charts, it was so strong in fact that I had to wonder if she was capable of making me happy all on her own.

She was barely done climaxing when I pulled her to me. I unzipped her dress and pulled it over her head. I looked down at her beautiful breasts then slid inside her hard. She wrapped her arms around my neck to hold on, pumping her hips, gripping me like a vise. I braced my arms on the edge of the desk for more leverage and pounded myself deeper inside her with each thrust. She felt incredible. She had a nice tight hot pussy that enveloped my cock. I could fuck her all night long and I would never be satisfied. Her pussy was like a drug to me and I couldn't get enough of her. She looked glorious with her long black hair and startling eyes as they zoned in on me. She looked so fuckable that I almost came inside of her.

I met her gaze and stared into her eyes, trying to convince her to trust me. I knew she only wanted me all to herself but I couldn't give her that. Not unless Carrie left me which I hoped would never happen. I hoped that Carrie would agree to an age old tradition and be happy with the life I had given her. It might be a lot to ask but a lot of the men that worked around me had mistresses that their wives were aware of. Just no one talked about it. It wasn't something that was out in the open for people to see. Cassandra however would have to be okay with it as well and she was starting to worry me as well.

I shook off these thoughts and tried to focus on the prize that I had in front of me. She pushed my breasts into my chest so I could feel her hard nipples against my smooth dress shirt. I reached around and grabbed her firm ass that flexed every time I pushed myself inside of her.

I rode her like that for a few minutes and I could feel her squeezing as another orgasm built up inside of her. I put my mouth over her breast, and sucked hard. She spread her legs wider for me so I could push further into her. She was moaning my name, and it was the sexiest sound on earth. I loved hearing her say my name when I was giving her so much pleasure. She wrapped her legs around me as she came. Moments later I pulled out of her and with a guttural cry my body shuddered as I released, creating milky ribbons all over her stomach.

Chapter Twenty-Two

Carrie

The wedding went off without a hitch of course; it was the wedding of the season in Paris. Although we tried to keep it small it didn't turn out that way. Last minute invite had gone out to the socialites of Paris and at the end of the day it turned out to be one hell of a party.

I went through the process in a fog. I had barely slept the night before after Cassandra had left. I had considered calling on Donna for some advice but at the end of the day I didn't want anything to come between me marrying the man of my dreams. Cassandra would have to be dealt with but in the meantime I wasn't about to just let her have my husband. Jeff came home late last night and I wondered if he had been with her that night. I couldn't bear to have him in bed with me after that so I left him a not that I would see him at the church.

I had a hard time feeling the wedded bliss however, my stomach churned the whole time. I couldn't help but keep my eye out on Cassandra and Jeff at the wedding. She of course was a guest as he had no idea I was aware of the two of them. Although Jeff remained professional towards her there was no denying that there was something between them. It was like electricity entered the room when they were together and I felt a stab of jealousy. I had a hard time believing that another girl could be better suited for Jeff than I was, we had always had so much fun together in the bedroom and yet I couldn't believe what I was seeing between them. I looked around the room at all the guests and I wondered how many of them knew about Cassandra. It was humiliating to think that you were the butt of some joke. I couldn't believe it myself and yet there it was, happening right before my eyes. I had a hard time believing that no one else knew about them. Did they think that our marriage was just a shame or did they think I was a stupid young bride who was in over my head? They were right I was. I hadn't even believed Donna when she said that Paris could be a problem for me.

At the reception Cassandra looked at me from time to time and I gave her a scathing look. I would not go down without a fight. This was not the 20's and I was not about to turn a blind eye to my husband's whims. I didn't care about the chemistry between the two of them. I knew that my husband loved me. I saw it in his eyes as he said his vows to me with tears in his eyes.

We left to Hawaii immediately for our honeymoon where we stayed for two weeks. It was like nothing had changed between us and I could only hope that he would completely forget about Cassandra when we returned home to Paris. Was that too much to ask?

We had sex every single night and some of the days that we were in Hawaii. It was like he couldn't quench himself from the thirst of me and I hoped that his thirst had everything to do with me and not for someone he missed.

The thought of returning home terrified me and yet there was no way around it. I would have to return to Paris where mistresses were the popular choice and hope that I could pull my husband away from his. If not I would have a hard decision to make. Stay with my husband even though I knew he was having an affair or return to the U.S. and start a life without him. The shame of it all may be too much especially once our father found out. But I needed to protect my heart over everything else and I just wasn't sure how much I could take. I despised Cassandra more than anything and to think that she had some kind of hold over the man I loved was a lot to bear. I always thought that it would just be Jeff and I growing old together. I thought he had only needed and wanted me but I had been wrong. Jeff allowed another woman to worm her way into our life. Now I had to deal with it and if I was honest with myself I really had no idea what to do. I was lost and it was my husband's fault.

Speak of the devil he came into the room just then. "How's my beautiful bride doing this morning? Are you ready to get back to the real world?"

146

I smiled weakly, "I'm not sure. It's been so nice like this just you and I."

"Yes it has been but it can't last forever."

"Why can't it? Aren't you happy with me?"

He looked at me as if trying to read my mind. "Is everything okay Carrie? You don't seem yourself."

I sighed deeply. I didn't want to get into things with Jeff on our honeymoon. Thinking about him and Cassandra was the last thing that I wanted to do. The situation truly seemed dire at times but I wasn't going to let her ruin our honeymoon.

"Is there something you would like to talk about?"

I looked at him then and it occurred to me that he was wondering if I knew about the affair. Was he offering to discuss the issue? I almost laughed at the thought. I shouldn't even be in the situation, never mind having to discuss it on my honeymoon. I had hoped that he would have realized that I was all he wanted and would have ended things with Cassandra. Maybe he had, I would only know when we returned to Paris and I was dreading it.

"No there is nothing that I want to talk about. I just want to enjoy my husband before we return to Paris and back to reality."

He smiled and came to where I was sitting on the couch in our hotel room. "Maybe I can do something to make you feel better."

I smiled. "Now that sounds wonderful husband."

"Mmmm...I like the sound of that."

"Me too."

We locked lips and it was like they lit on fire. God, he was such a good kisser. We kissed, our tongues teasing one another as I began taking off his shirt. I sucked on his tongue gently and he ripped at my robe, undoing the belt and letting it fall to my feet. He began pawing at my breasts. I knew I was driving him wild and I sort of liked it. Our hands were all over each other as I unbuttoned his shirt and tore it off. I loved being near Jeff I couldn't get enough of his mouth. I craved every inch of him.

147

"Suck my cock Carrie, suck it really good."

I got down on my knees and took him into my mouth. I sucked on his hard cock while I played with his balls. He was groaning above me his hands in my hair. I moaned as I licked his shaft with my tongue and circled it around his shaft. He moaned my name and I just sucked harder. My tongue twirled around the tip of his cock and all I could think about at that moment was pleasing him as best I could. Screw Cassandra. This was my man and I knew exactly how to please him. My tongue rubbed up against his shaft as I sucked on his cock. I could tell by the way he was tugging on my hair that he was horny and about to come undone.

Jeff pulled me up from him and picked me up into his arms, I loved when he did that, it was one of the sexiest things about him. He craved me like I craved him and it was as if his animal instincts kicked in. He carried me over to the bed and laid me down. He looked down at me with a heat in his eyes I had seen many times before. He then climbed on top of me and spread my legs. Jeff admired my pussy as if he couldn't wait to lick me. I was already wet, the experience for me was highly erotic and it was actually quite easy to forget that we had any problems to deal with.

Jeff bent down and put his mouth on my pussy. I closed my eyes, enjoying every moment of his tongue as it lapped at me over and over again. I moaned as he tasted my pussy. He was licking and sucking and it made me dizzy. He was so good at licking my pussy that I didn't want him to stop. Fuck the rest of the positioning; I wanted his tongue inside me all day. He definitely knew what he was doing when it came to oral sex. He began to suck on my clit while he pushed two fingers inside me. I moaned loudly as the sensations felt so incredible. Waves of pleasure coursed through me and I moaned again as I came against his fingers. He pumped his fingers inside me harder as he tickled my pussy with his tongue. Jeff was finger fucking me really good and I felt myself going a little bit mad from all the pleasure.

"Fuck me Jeff please."

148

He took his fingers out of me and went into the X-Factor position. I loved the fact that he always liked to try new things with me. Sex was always a surprise. It started off in the missionary position and that's when he slid his cock inside me. I moaned with his cock pumping inside of me. He then moved so that his chest and legs were no longer on my body and he formed an X with my body. I was able to feel more of his movement in that position, I was also able to grab a hold of his hot ass. He excited me so much I could barely contain myself.

Jeff moved inside me slowly, it wasn't the kind of position for fast fucking. He thrust into me a few more times before pulling his cock out of me.

He lay down onto the couch and I prepared myself to ride on his big cock. I straddled him on top but this time I was facing his feet in the reverse cowgirl position. It was a delicious position because he was incredibly deep and I had all the control. I chose to ride him hard until an orgasm so intense rocked my body causing me to collapse at his feet shaking until it was over. Jeff pulled me to him with a smile on his face. I rolled over until I was lying on the couch on my side. He spooned me in the same position and slipped his cock in from behind. I moaned as he went in deep and began to rock his cock inside me. He picked up the pace and began fucking me hard with his cock inside me deep. It was an intense sensation and I closed my eyes enjoying the thickness of his cock and how it filled me up perfectly. I pushed my ass against him and met each one of his thrusts with the same urgency he was giving me. I pounded my ass into his cock loving how hard he felt when he thrust in deep inside me. I groaned wantonly loving his cock so much that I would have fucked Jeff all day if he asked me to. I felt another orgasm building up inside of me. This time it was coming slow and I gave myself in to it. It climbed with me and I ached to explode all over Jeff's cock. I hoped that we could orgasm together, it just made things that much more intense when I was with Jeff.

"Come with me baby. Please cum inside me."

He groaned and continued to push inside me deeply. He fucked me even harder and when I screamed out his name he spilled inside me at the same time. We fit so well together.

We lay there in our post-orgasmic bliss and held unto each other. I loved Jeff so much that I hoped things would only get better between us. I wanted us to be stronger together, to get through anything and do it all just the two of us.

Jeff started to trail his finger along my birth mark and I smiled softly. It was our bond, our mark that joined us together.

"What are you thinking about babe?"

He sighed, "Nothing. I just love you Carrie. I hope you know that."

"I do. I always do."

Chapter Twenty-Three
Carrie

Upon our return to Paris things basically went back to the way they had been before. Jeff's hours weren't as crazy as they had been before but he still spent a lot of time in the office. At least I now knew why. He wasn't there working hard and being stressed out like I had imagined. No he was taking every opportunity that he could to spend time with Cassandra. That was where I saw the problem to be. Wasn't the wife the one that was supposed to get the most time in these situations? Wasn't it the mistress that had to be on the back burner? But that wasn't the case. It was me who hardly saw my husband. When we did we normally had "quickie" sex, the long lovemaking sessions seemed to be a thing of the past. He still lied to me about the affair as well. It was always that "things were so busy" at work or that he need to work late to finish a report. There was always some work related reason he couldn't return home to me.

I was at a loss as to what to do. I didn't want to talk about it with any of my friends because I found it terribly embarrassing. If I told Donna it would only be a confirmation of what she already expected to happen. I should have listened to her. Maybe Jeff and I could have moved somewhere else in Europe. Somewhere where mistresses weren't seen as such a freeing experience for the men. Though if I was going to be really honest with myself Jeff probably would have found someone anywhere that we moved. He was obviously missing something in our relationship that he was getting from Cassandra. If I gave him everything then why would he feel the need to step out? He would feel fulfilled with me and clearly he did not. I didn't know what to do about that fact. It stung more than I wanted to admit. I had always thought that I would fall in love and that would be it for me. I always believed that when I married I would be everything that my husband ever wanted. The thought that Jeff wanted something that I couldn't give him was devastating. It wasn't like we didn't have an outgoing and open sex life. I had always been willing to try new things so he wasn't with Cassandra because she was freakier so to speak. So what was it about Cassandra that drew Jeff in, what was she giving him that made him long to be with her more often than he was with me? I couldn't know. I wouldn't have these answers unless I spoke with him and at the moment I was just unwilling to do that.

I feared the choice, the ultimatum. Cassandra had walked into my life so easily and confidently that I wondered if there was a chance that Jeff preferred her to me. If I confronted him and demanded he make a choice, I worried that he wouldn't choose me. And then what? Armed with the knowledge that my new husband didn't truly want me, where would I go? I would be lost. Forced to return to America and the tired "I told you so," that I was sure to get from my father. It was almost too much to bear. I did not want to prove my father right. I had always believed he was wrong about Jeff and I. I thought that he had no idea what he was talking about. We were in love and we belong together. Right? Did we belong together? I had to wonder now as my husband carried on with another woman. Maybe I had been wrong all along, maybe we both had. Until I had some sort of a backup plan I had no intention of confronting Jeff. I didn't want to end up the woman scorned, left with nothing. I wanted to be confident I would win before sending Cassandra away.

I sat on the couch in our apartment sipping on wine. I had no idea if Jeff was going to make an appearance that evening or not. I had decided that I would demand that he come home more often and see how he would react to that before confronting him about Cassandra. If he was going to have a mistress I was not going to suffer because of it. Cassandra would need to take a back seat to the scenario. I shook my head unable to believe that these were things that I actually had to consider.

There was one thing that was certain however and that was that my life had become increasingly boring since Jeff started spending time with Cassandra. We didn't have sex nearly enough as I desired and it was often short and sweet. I wanted more. I was too young to be sitting at home alone all the time. I was living in one of the most beautiful cities in the world and yet I had nothing to do. I missed my husband and I found that I was getting lonelier by the day. It sucked being away from him especially when I knew he was with someone else. I hadn't lived there long enough to make any real friends. That would probably have to change if I had any hope of being happy.

Just then there was a knock on the door. I cringed hoping that it wasn't Cassandra making a post-wedding visit in the hopes of getting me out of Jeff's life. I made my way to the door and opened it.

Standing on the other side was Jeff's adoptive father Curtis. He was the one that was responsible for teaching Jeff all about business and made him the success he was today. He was a wealthy man himself and always hoped that Jeff would take over things for him. Instead Jeff had wanted to make something for himself. They had a great relationship and I almost envied the fact that Jeff grew up with someone like that instead of our father who had not been easy on me one bit while growing up.

"Hello there Carrie, how are you this evening?"

I smiled warmly at him. "I'm great Curtis. How are you? I'm just having a glass of wine. Would you like to come in for one?"

I opened the door wider for him to enter and he followed me back to the living room. I went and retrieved another glass and poured him some wine. I was grateful for the company so that I wouldn't have to drink alone. I hadn't spent a whole lot of time with Curtis before but I knew him to be a good kind man. He had raised Jeff right and I was grateful for that. Curtis was a handsome man for his age. I had never noticed before.

"I would love to. Is Jeff around? I wanted to speak with him about something."

"No, I'm afraid he's not. He's still at the office."

"Is he? I was just there and was told he was gone for the day."

We sat there on the couch with an awkward silence hanging in the air. He had caught me off guard and I had no idea how to reply. So Jeff wasn't at work that much was obvious. So was he spending the night with Cassandra? My face burned suddenly with embarrass-ment. Humiliated right in front of my father-in-law was not exactly what I wanted. I wonder if he knew about his son and that thought just made my face burn that much brighter. How could Jeff do this to me?

"Is everything okay Carrie?"

My eyes fluttered back up to his. I hoped that he couldn't tell how embarrassed I was about the whole situation. I couldn't possibly confide in him, it would be just too mortifying.

"Yes, of course. Everything is fine."

"How have things been since the wedding?"

I paused. Curtis obviously knew something. I sipped the wine and held myself back from pouring the whole bottle into my glass.

"Jeff's been really busy with work and I guess it's been a little hard on me. I never see him and our honeymoon was the most at-tention I have had in months. I don't know what to do."

"Is there someone else Carrie?"

"What do you mean?"

"Do you believe that my son is seeing someone else? I hate to be so crass, but it's so obvious that something is wrong. If I can help I would like to."

"There's nothing you can do I'm afraid."

"So it is true."

Tears welled up in my eyes as I nodded. "She actually came to my door and asked me not to marry Jeff. It was one of the most humil-iating experiences of my life. I don't know what to do. I don't want to confront Jeff because I'm afraid he might leave me."

He smiled at me warmly. "Jeff could never leave you Carrie, de-spite your tangled past, you are an extraordinary woman. He knows that trust me. He's just in over his head here with the lifestyle of Paris. I can't say that I agree with what he is doing but I don't think that he's trying to hurt you."

"But he is and what does he expect me to do about it?"

Curtis took a sip of his wine and studied me for a moment. "I don't have the answer to that Carrie. I've never had an affair myself. Paris is certainly different and people do take a little more than they should but you have to decide what you want in life and what you're willing to put up with."

"I love him. I just wish I was enough."

"You are. But you still have to decide what you want Carrie. Are you okay with letting him have what he wants or do you want something different for your life?"

"I don't know. I'm so lost right now."

He grabbed my hand and gave it a squeeze. I felt understood finally for the first time in a long time. I had needed to talk about it, I just felt humiliated. But he was right I needed to figure out what I wanted for myself and whether or not I would be okay with being in a marriage that included a mistress. I knew I hated the idea but it seemed to be the norm in Paris and what could I do about that?

"I want to be his only one. I always have but I just don't feel like he wants the same thing. He sought her out because she offered him something that I obviously couldn't."

"That may not be the case at all."

I looked at Curtis with new eyes. He seemed so sweet and understanding. It all seemed so logical through his eyes. Why couldn't Jeff be more like his dad? Why did he have to do things to hurt me?

Without thinking I leaned over and kissed him. He didn't stop me and when my lips touched his, there just seemed something right about the whole thing. I didn't stop it and neither did he. For the first time in a long time I finally felt needed by someone. I had no idea where my husband was but he clearly had no interest in sleeping with me. He was taking his need out on another woman.

Curtis was handsome and distinguished in a Cary grant sort of way. His mouth melted underneath mine and when I felt his tongue touch my lips I felt like I had been zapped by electricity. My whole body warmed to my genuine surprise. I had not expected to feel this way for anyone but Jeff but I didn't want to think of Jeff at the moment. He was off somewhere not thinking about me, so maybe it was time I started thinking of myself as well.

Curtis moved to me and pushed me back onto the couch. I smiled as he came in for another kiss. He was sexy in his pursuit. He climbed up on top of me and I gasped as I felt his erection pushed up against me. I could not believe what was happening. He just came to take whatever he wanted from me and I was powerless to stop it. The truth was I didn't want to stop it. My loneliness had taken over and I wanted more than anything to feel needed and wanted again; to be possessed once again by a man with desire. Well I could stop it, I probably should stop it but I didn't really want to. Maybe I had too much wine or maybe I was just sick of waiting for my husband to realize what a selfish jerk he was being. Either way I didn't care. I wanted Curtis in that moment.

He pulled off my tank top and his mouth plunged onto my nipple. I wasn't wearing a bra so he had easy access. He sucked hard causing my nipple to stiffen hard. I was breathless beneath him and as he sucked on my nipples I felt my pussy grow wet. Curtis kissed me fiercely on the mouth his tongue slipping inside my mouth. I moaned as our tongues touched and our kisses grew more passionate. I undid my jeans and slid out of them. His hand slid down into my bikini panties and he found my clit. My pussy had grown wet and his fingers slid easily over my clit. He found my opening and slid two fingers inside of me and I moaned loudly. God he was so hot. I had not expected Curtis to be so forward and intense.

He began kissing my body starting from my nipples trailing all the way down my body. He circled my navel and continued down to my bikini line. He kissed my pussy right through my panties. He was driving me slowly crazy and I loved it. I looked down at him with longing and waited impatiently as he continued to kiss my pussy. Curtis wasn't paying attention to me at all, he was comple-

156

ly focused on his task and he went ahead and pulled down my panties. His tongue licked at the sides of my opening and my eyes fluttered shut.

"Oh Curtis that feels so good." It occurred to me that Jeff could walk through the door at any moment but I didn't care. Let him see what he did to me. He could hardly be mad at me after what he had been up to.

He sucked on my clit and continued licking my pussy like it was an ice cream cone. I ached for him; I wanted to have him inside me immediately. I felt dizzy as he licked my pussy as slowly as possible.

My pussy was already throbbing in want for his cock. Curtis made me ache to be fucked by him even though it wasn't supposed to be like this. But I didn't care what Jeff thought anymore, I wanted Curtis to fuck me and I didn't care that he was Jeff's father. I needed to have his cock inside me, pumping into me over and over again.

His hands were on my breasts kneading them and I moaned when he pinched one of my nipples. My hand found his cock already hard as a rock. I squeezed it hard thinking about what it could do to me. How good it was going to feel inside of me. I had completely lost focus of what I was doing; all I could see was Curtis. He pulled me up from the couch. We were standing up in front of each other and he lifted one of my legs up to his waist. I circled that leg around his waist and held on to him. Curtis would have to support my weight for the most part as he held onto the leg around his waist. I was left standing on one leg as he entered me. They guy was ridiculously flexible for his age. We were incredibly close and when he pushed into me his mouth found mine as well. He nipped at my bottom lip and the action caused me to grow even hornier. God I could not wait for him to bend me over, it was all I could think about.

Curtis moved inside of me flawlessly and I moaned with every thrust. He kissed my lips and then moved down to my jawline and then my neck. He pumped his cock inside me rhythmically making

157

my pussy wet. He bit my neck and it caused me to grip him tighter around the waist.

"Okay sweetheart, time for a switch. I want to do some fucking."

I grinned at his words; I never would have thought he would say such a thing to me. He pulled out and twirled me around in one quick motion. With my back to him he put his hand against my back and bent me over. Excitement built up inside of me as I anticipated his cock sliding into me hard and deep. He took both of my wrists and pulled them behind my back. It supported me enough that I could bend all the way over so that my head met my feet. He plunged into me causing me to cry out. The positioning made it feel like he was so much deeper and so much bigger. The position tightened me up so that there was more friction between us. He felt enormous inside of me and my pussy dripped with pleasure.

"Oh Curtis, your cock is so big."

"You like that don't you darling. You like being fucked by my big cock?"

"Oh yes. Please fuck me harder."

With that, I got exactly what I asked for. He pounded against my ass over and over again, his cock buried deep inside of me. He was so deep that I could feel his balls slapping up against me.

"Oh god, that feels good. Oh Curtis you fuck me so good."

I knew I was going to cum hard, it was inevitable. He was pounding my pussy so good. It was a hard rough sex and I was powerless against his thrust because he held my arms back so that I was constantly pressed against him. I felt the buildup coming inside of me, my pussy tightened around his cock as he continued to pound against my ass.

I cried out as I exploded on his cock.

"Oh god, oh god I'm coming."

He slowed his pumping down and released one of my hands. Curtis bent down and his fingers found my clit. I moaned as he rubbed

158

hard against my clit. Everything was ultra-sensitive after my orgasm so the sensation was thrilling.

Curtis slid out of me and pulled me up by my other hand. I was a little out of sorts from my orgasm but I followed him as he led me to the kitchen counter. He pushed me up against it and I braced myself against the counter. I bent over, my ass pointed into the air. I heard him groan and it wasn't so much a groan as it was a growl. He couldn't wait to fuck me and he made me aware of that when he plunged inside me once again. He went in deep and the hardness of his cock left me immobilized. He was incredibly gifted with the length and girth of is cock and every inch of him was filling me up to perfection.

"Fuck me Curtis. Fuck me hard."

A little roughness never hurt anyone and I was so beyond horny at that point that I just wanted him to bury himself in me deep and fuck me hard.

Curtis pounded inside of me and I turned around to look at him. He was gorgeous with his tanned skin and jet black hair; he was an incredibly handsome man. Thank god he looked nothing like Jeff that would have been a little weird. I watched him as he fucked me and the sight of him pounding into me drove me insane. I came again onto his cock and I cried out with pleasure. Oh but I wasn't done, I wanted more so much more. He took me away from the counter and bent me further over. He was positioning me for the wheelbarrow. I braced myself on the floor with my two hands. Once he saw that I was ready he lifted my legs off the floor. Not once did his cock leave me, he stayed steady inside me and wrapped my legs around his waist. I locked my feet into position behind his back and held on for dear life. It was definitely going to be an intense workout on my arms as I balanced myself up. Curtis pushed inside me deeper, slowly at first and then building up momentum. He was able to get so much deeper with that position and I moaned loudly as he pumped inside me faster. Waves of pleasure just took over my whole body to the point where I could barely think.

"You feel so good Carrie; your pussy is so nice and tight. You feel incredible."

"I need your cock Curtis, god you feel good."

"You want my cum Carrie? Tell me you want me to pump your pussy full of cum?"

I moaned eagerly and he thrust inside me harder and faster as I felt myself losing control. He cried out as well when he spilled inside me. Curtis slowed down his thrusts and slowly let my legs down from him.

Curtis helped me up off the floor and kissed my hand.

"Fuck that was good Carrie."

*∗∗

I was lying on the couch when Jeff finally made his way home. I didn't look at him the entire time he moved around the living room, putting things away and taking his jacket off.

"How was work? You just left now?"

"Yeah, it was a crazy day. I'm sorry I hope you weren't bored. What did you get up to tonight?"

I smiled, "Oh I think I found myself a new hobby. Something to keep me busy while you are working so hard."

Chapter Twenty-Four

It's amazing just how easy it is to get tangled up in a situation that you never thought you would find yourself in before. I had been outraged to find out my new husband had taken on a mistress, even though he pledged his love to me every single day. I loved my husband with every fiber in my body. I would never have dreamed it was possible to deliberately hurt him. But lines that were never supposed to be crossed got harder to see. The things I never thought were possible for me suddenly became possible.

I had waited too many nights at home waiting for him to return from work while fully knowing he had never worked late at all. Cassandra was the reason why he never came home. At first I was hurt and torn about leaving him. I wondered how our lives had gotten to that point. There was a time when Jeff and I were so in love. It never would have occurred to either of us to cheat. But things had happened between us that had changed everything, possibly forever. I had no idea what was going to happen in the future but what I did know was that my husband and I were both living different lives. We were more apart now than ever.

Things just continually got worse for the two of them. Together anyways. It appeared as if the more time we spent together the less we wanted to or maybe that was just my impression of things. I missed Jeff more than anything but he was home less and less as the months went by and I was powerless to do anything about it. I wanted to be near him but it was hard to maintain when he was always with Cassandra.

The night I was with Curtis had been one of the best nights I had ever experienced in some time. Never would I have thought a man like Curtis would be so damn fun to play with. I had never imagined that sleeping with an older man could be so satisfying. But there it was. Jeff was out getting his cake and damn well eating it too so why should it be any different for me? I was tired of being so lonely all the time. I wanted to be loved and desired. Sex sure wouldn't hurt either. But Jeff was unwilling or unable to do that for me so I was determined to continue to live my life anyways.

I rolled over in my bed and saw the outline of Curtis under the quilt. He had a nice strong back and I began to rub it. Jeff was out of town so I had no worries that he would walk in on us. We had been sleeping together for a few weeks now and the more time I spent with him the less I cared what Jeff would think about it. After all, he was too busy sleeping with Cassandra and at the rate they were going I should have let Jeff go off with her instead. I thought that my husband had my best interests at heart but I was starting to wonder if he even loved me at all anymore.

I began to kiss Curtis's back until he groaned awake beside me. He turned to me and smiled.

"Hi beautiful."

I smiled back at him. "Hi there."

"Is everything okay?"

"Yes, why do you ask?" I bent over and kissed him.

"Just the way you are looking at me."

"Do you ever feel bad? I mean. He is your son. You raised him from birth. Sometimes I think we are crazy for what we are doing, don't you?"

"I know what you are saying sweetheart. But Jeff betrayed you first. He isn't even here. He's out of town and conveniently he took his assistant with him. Are you even confident that it's a business trip or just a vacation with his new girlfriend?"

"Stop, don't say that."

"I'm not trying to hurt you Carrie. But it's the truth. Now what's happening to us is very different. We should be together. You know that. When it comes down to it Jeff is going to leave. You guys don't even have a real marriage anymore. He ruined that. So I don't think you should feel guilty any longer. Let's just enjoy what's happening between us and the rest will just work itself out."

His mouth seared against mine and I couldn't help but moan with his proximity to me. He could make me so horny so quickly. I really couldn't get enough.

"I want you to sit on my cock Carrie and show me what you can do to me."

I groaned as I felt his cock through his boxer shorts. Curtis was rock hard and I wanted to sit on him. My pussy was throbbing and I ached to grind against his cock. We had spent a lot of time in the bedroom since we met.

He slid a hand up my thigh. I was wet already and a smile came across his face when his fingers slid into me. God it felt so good.

"No underwear Carrie? You are one naughty girl."

"Maybe." I said breathlessly. "Maybe I'm just a tease."

"Oh no. Believe me there won't be any teasing. Just good fucking."

He slid my t-shirt up and exposed my breasts. His hands grabbed my ass and he squeezed.

"You have a great ass."

I giggled. Being with Curtis was exciting and I loved the way that he made me feel.

I sat up on the bed. He picked me up then and I wrapped my legs around his waist. Our mouths found each other once again and I sucked on his tongue gently. The fog had descended on me again and all I could see and feel was Curtis all around me. I was drugged once again and I wouldn't have had it any other way.

I lifted myself briefly so he could take off his shorts. When he was naked from the waist down he impaled me unto his cock. From that angle his big cock pushed into me deeply and I cried out happily. God, he felt so good. I took control at that moment and rode his cock well until he groaned. I placed my hands on his shoulders and ground myself against his cock. The waves of pleasure that came through me were crazy good.

"You were right Carrie; you are a really good fuck."

I giggled as I picked up the pace and I rode him good. I could tell he was trying hard to control his orgasm so I slowed down again. As I rode him slowly my hands went to my breasts and I fondled myself before him. He watched me with a small smile on his lips and an intense heat in his eyes.

"Fuck you are so hot."

"Fuck me."

"Oh I plan on fucking you really good baby."

He picked me up once again and rose from the bed. I bent down on the floor with my forearms ahead of me. I raised my hips so that my ass stuck up high in the air. Curtis came up behind me and plunged himself into me from behind. He was incredibly deep so much so that I thought I might pass out with pleasure with every thrust he gave me. I exploded onto his cock and called out his name when I did so. He continued to pound himself against my ass as another orgasm took a hold of my body. I was consumed by pleasure and I closed my eyes and took it all in. His cock filled me up completely and hit every nerve that I possessed.

"Oh god, I'm going to cum." A third orgasm ripped through me as I moaned loudly. He fucked me roughly and it just caused me to want even more.

Curtis pulled himself out of me and I tried to focus on getting into position for a difficult angle. He rolled me over until I was lying on my back. He grabbed both of my legs and pushed them up in the air and then pushed them forward towards my head. My ankles fell on either side of my head and I was in awe of how flexible I was. Man, this one was going to be really good. He stood above me looking down at me and not once did he break eye contact with me. It was one of the most erotic experiences of my life. He went into position and squatted about me dipping his cock into me over and over again. The blood was starting to rush to my head which gave me a dizzying feeling. Oddly enough it increased the pleasure that I was feeling every time his cock pushed into me. I moaned feeling greedy for his cock. I needed him now; I wanted his cock more than anything. He continued to pump his cock into me in quick succession. When he came in me I felt heady from being upside down for that period of time.

Curtis slipped his cock out of me and grabbed hold of my ankles, pulling them down towards him once again. I was breathing heavily and just laid there while he looked down at me.

"That was fucking hot. You my girl are so hot. It makes me want to go round two with you all over again." He was smiling down at me.

I laughed, "I'm not sure I could handle another round."

"Oh I think you would like taking my cock another round."

My face grew crimson in color as I smiled back up at him. He stood up once again and held his hand out to me. I grasped onto it, allowing him to pull me up.

"You're so sexy Curtis."

I got up from the bed. "I'm going to take a bath; you are welcome to join me."

He smiled as I walked out of the room. I watched as the bathtub filled with water while sitting on the edge of the tub. I went back into my bedroom and laid my clothes out on the bed to prepare for the day. I headed back to the tub and stepped gently into the hot water. It felt glorious against my skin. As I lay down in the tub the heat just melted away the soreness and stiffness from my body. There was nothing more relaxing than a bubble bath; it just eased the stress away immediately. The hotter the better, that was the way that I like my bathes. The water cooled down so quickly that it was best to start it off hot. I looked up as Curtis entered the bathroom. He looked down at me with lustful eyes. A smile came across my face when I saw him step into the bath to join me. He was carrying two wine glasses. It was the perfect thought.

"You look so lovely covered in bubbles Carrie."

I took down the shower head and turned it on. All I could think about was Curtis's cock and I wanted to make myself feel good. I had wine and a bathtub, why not play a little bit? I loved getting

Curtis aroused. He sat down in the bathwater and his legs moved to either side of me. He handed me a glass and I took a delicate sip.

I didn't want an orgasm necessarily; I would leave that for Curtis to take care of later on. I knew he would do a good job of it and he would probably give me multiple orgasms. I just wanted to feel good. I was a little horny thinking about Curtis and I couldn't help but play with my pussy a little.

I put the shower head against my clit and turned it up, careful not to push water directly inside of me. Curtis kept his eyes on me the entire time. I could tell he was getting really turned on. The water tickled at my clit and I massaged the water against my pussy. I leaned back against the tub and closed my eyes. Waves of pleasure came over me and I moaned. I almost couldn't wait to see what Curtis had in store for me. He knew exactly what to do to make me feel good. I slid two fingers inside my pussy as the water continued to tickle my clit. I finger fucked myself slowly and then a little faster. I moaned again feeling incredible. I was capable of making myself feel just as good as a man could; it was just more fun having a man around. I felt an orgasm build up and I let myself go. "Oh!" It felt amazing letting go of pleasure and allowing myself to experience it all. I got an orgasm after all.

I turned the shower head off and attached it back to the tub. I leaned back against the tub and took a sip of my wine. Curtis moved in and pulled me in for a passionate kiss.

Chapter Twenty-Five

When Jeff returned home from his trip away he seemed even more distant than he was before he left. That was saying a lot since we weren't doing very well to begin with. I was at a loss once again. From what I understood about mistresses in Paris was that they were taken as sort of a side dish; never the main course. The wife always got the most of everything and the mistress had to be satisfied with whatever was left over. But that was not the case at all in our situation. Cassandra seemed to be taking up most of the time, whereas I rarely saw my husband. It wasn't fair and to be honest it was becoming a little insulting. Did he really still believe that I had no idea what was going on? Did he really think that I thought that he was work that whole time? He was treating me like a fool and I was getting sick of it.

I was preparing dinner on an evening since he had been home from work early for a change. I was making a Bolognese sauce that would pair nicely with the wine he had brought in that night.

"Hey sweetheart, how was your day?"

I barely looked up at him as I stirred the sauce lazily in the pot. He came around and kissed me on the cheek. "My day was great. Your father took me to the University in the area and I got enrolled to a fashion design program. I can't wait. It's the most exciting thing that has happened to me."

He looked at me strangely, "More exciting than our wedding day?"

I snorted, "Our wedding day was exciting but not much afterwards seemed to have been." To hell with it I was opening up the bottle of wine before dinner. He watched me as I popped the cork and poured a single glass of wine. I drank half of it before I set it down on the counter.

"What is that supposed to mean? Are you mad at me because you seem awfully hostile right now?"

I chuckled, mainly to avoid crying. "I seem hostile? Why do you think that might be?" I looked him dead in the eye while I sipped my wine. His eyes narrowed and I wondered if he was going to finally confess.

"I have no idea why you would be upset Carrie. I have given you a great life. You have all the freedom you want, you have the ability to go to a great school and start a career in fashion. What more do you want from me?"

"How about your time? Can I have that? I never see you anymore Jeff. I thought coming to Paris was supposed to make our lives better and yet we don't see each other. I would have preferred to stay in the US and deal with our father's wrath rather than lose you like this."

It was the first time I had seen Jeff look even remotely guilty. It was just a flash though however and the look was gone. Poof! Right before my eyes.

"You know I am swamped with the restructuring of the division. I have been working my ass off. But it's not forever Carrie. Once things slow down I will have lots of time to spend with you. It's just bad timing."

I looked him dead in the eyes and said, "You're lying."

Taken aback he didn't even know how to respond. Instead he just stared at me in shock. I had never spoken to him in this manner before. I had always just followed his lead in everything he wanted to do. Paris had been a mistake, I knew that now. I should have forced him to deal with our father and to put me first. Instead we had moved out of the country and I still managed to end up alone.

"I know." I hissed at him.

His eyes widened. "Know what?" He asked the question but there was no authority behind it. He was afraid that he already knew the answer to his question.

"I know about your mistress. You must have really thought I was stupid."

He stood there stunned. "How did you know? Oh god, I'm sorry. That's not even the right question to ask. Carrie it hasn't been going on that long. I just felt lonely and I was spending so much time at the office."

I couldn't believe he was standing there lying to me.

"Oh really? I guess Cassandra didn't mention to you that she had stopped by the night before our wedding to ask me not to marry you."

He looked like he had been slapped. Cassandra had clearly never mentioned such a thing to him. "I had no idea. I'm sorry she should never have come here."

"Imagine how I must feel Jeff. Looking forward to marrying the man of my dreams only to have his slut show up at the door and remind me that you don't feel the same way."

"That's not true. I love you."

"You have a funny way of showing it. You have been with her this whole time while I have sat home alone for so many nights. Is that love?"

He stared at me again, unable to speak. I could imagine the torment that was going through him right then. I knew it because I felt exactly the same way. I turned off the stove and walked away from him.

"You don't need to worry about me asking for a divorce. I plan on getting everything that I want out of this situation. Say hi to Cassandra for me though."

I walked out the door and headed for Curtis's place. When his front door swung open I landed in his arms. He knew that something was wrong but he didn't say a word.

He pulled me to the kitchen where he was also preparing for dinner. Curtis grabbed me by the waist and lifted me up on the counter. His lips found mine and we kissed, our tongues finding one another. We were making out pretty hard and spices were getting all over us. I could have cared less all I wanted was his lips on mine. He sucked on my tongue a little and I moaned softly. He was so incredibly hot, I could barely stand it. This was what I needed at the moment.

"So, what should we do first?" I whispered.

He flashed me a devilish grin that made me warm all over. "Oh my darling Carrie, I'm going to make you feel really good. I hope you don't mind if I do dirty things to you."

I gasped, "God no, in fact I expect it." Everything about Curtis was intoxicating and I couldn't get enough of his lips and the voice he used when he talked dirty to me was enough to send a lady to the mental hospital.

Curtis leaned in and slipped his hand around my neck pulling me in to him as his mouth claimed mine once again. He tasted sweet and alluring. His mouth was hot to the touch and I almost moaned from his kisses. He kissed me softly at first and then his kisses became more fevered as if he needed my mouth on his. Who was I kidding, I needed it too. His tongue slipped into my mouth and I claimed it. I sucked him slowly, tasting him before I pulled away. He pulled me in again as he was not finished kissing me. His tongue found mine again and our kisses grew more passionate. I touched his face and there must have been flour on my hands as I left a flour print on his cheek. I giggled and licked at his lips.

His hand found my breast and he kneaded it softly; leaving flour on my shirt. He began pulling off my t-shirt and tossing it aside. He stopped kissing me momentarily to look down at my breasts that were dying to be released from my bra. He looked back up at me with a smile on his face.

"You are so beautiful Carrie, do you have any idea?"

I smiled though all I could think about was what he looked like naked. I knew what he looked like naked but I wanted to see him again. I wanted all of him and I could barely stand to wait. He unclasped my bra and he pushed me back until I was lying down on

170

the counter, one with the flour. His mouth found my nipple and he sucked, nipped and licked it. The sensation I was getting was making my panties wet. I moaned softly as he replaced his mouth with his fingers and pulled on my nipple causing an ache between my legs. I liked it; it made me horny. He continued playing with my nipples causing me to moan as a pleasure built up in my body. My hand reached down and I massaged the front of his pants, I could feel his hard cock pushing against his pants. He smiled down at me.

"Baby, I want to suck your cock so badly. It's all I have been able to think about."

"God, that is so hot Carrie, you can suck my cock anytime you want to."

I nodded, still speechless by the things that came out of his mouth. I felt wanton around him, he possessed me and my body needed him like my lungs needed air to breathe. To have him please my body, to give me what I wanted, that's all I could think about. He undid his button and pulled the zipper on his pants down. Curtis brought his pants down to his knees and slid his underwear down with them. He hard cock bounced before me now free from his underwear. He was so thick; the sight was always breathtaking to me. His thick cock made me wet and I ached for it to be inside me. He straddled me and I took his cock into my mouth and sucked on it. His eyes closed above me and I sucked hard while I massaged his balls. My tongue began to swirl against his shaft and then around his tip. He moaned with eagerness and I sucked him even harder.

"Oh Carrie, it's so good. Oh baby I love when you suck my cock, you're so good at it."

I took his cock deeper into my mouth until it hit the back of my throat. I moved up and down rhythmically until I moved fluidly with him in my mouth.

His moans excited me and I felt my pussy become even wetter. He pulled his cock out of my mouth and finished undressing himself, tossing his shirt aside. I followed suit and undid my jeans and slipped them off. I was only wearing a thong underneath so it was

171

easy to dispose of. He watched me undress and he couldn't take his eyes off my pussy.

"I think I need to taste some pussy now baby."

He slid off of me and spread my legs for me. I wanted him between my legs; I wanted him to lick my pussy. He looked so sexy there in between my legs, looking down at my pussy.

Curtis dropped down before me and licked my pussy slowly as if he was enjoying a good meal. I moaned loudly as he licked up and down slowly. It felt incredible as his tongue licked the sides of my opening, causing a tingle to run through my body. He took my clit in his mouth and sucked on it causing me to moan loudly as my pussy dripped. He flicked my clit with his tongue and I thought I might lose my mind.

"Oh god Curtis...oh god...please...that feels so good."

He looked up and smiled, "Do you like that baby?"

"Oh god yes it feels incredible."

My pussy was dripping and he was licking it up, tasting every inch of me. I felt the buildup coming. I was going to cum right there in his mouth.

"Oh god, oh wow, I'm going to cum."

"Let me taste you baby, I can't wait." Curtis was sucking on my clit when he buried a finger inside my pussy and started pumping away. The feeling was incredible and I cried out softly as I had an orgasm so delicious that I wanted even more. I needed him, all of him.

"How was that?"

I just grinned with desire written all over my face.

He grabbed my legs and pulled me off of the counter. Once my feet hit the floor he spun me around so that I was facing the counter. He pushed me against it and I bent over. I couldn't have been more turned on. You would think that Curtis was a young man for all the moves he had. But he definitely had the experience required to make me happy.

"Do you like doggy sweetheart? I'm going to fuck you so good you won't be able to walk for a week."

I grinned, loving the sound of his words. I was in position and waiting for him to plunge his cock inside of me. He was pushed right up against my ass and the feeling made me just about lose my mind. He plunged inside me fast and hard.

I was rendered speechless as he started moving slowly. He felt fantastic and he started pounding his smooth cock even harder inside me. He was moaning softly as well and it was making me lose control. His body pushed against my ass and I looked over my shoulder. Curtis looked so sexy fucking me and I smiled up at him.

"Mmmm, you sexy girl. You feel delicious. You should see the incredible view I have of your sexy little ass."

I moaned, his voice, his words, his cock were driving me mad. And just when I thought it couldn't get any better he reached around and started playing with my clit. It was almost too much to bear, I couldn't get enough. I was moaning softly wanting to beg for more but feeling already possessed by him. My pussy was so wet, he was driving me wild. "Oh god, Curtis, your cock feels amazing."

"Just relax sweetheart." I gasped as pleasure coursed through me. He continued pumping his cock inside me as an orgasm took a hold of me once again. "Oh god Curtis, oh god that feels so good, I can't get enough of you." I whispered to him as my breath caught.

"I love having my cock in you. Let's try something else."

Curtis pulled his cock out of me and turned me around. I waited to see what he had in mind.

His cock, oh god, looking at his size made me horny all over again. I wanted to be fucked by him desperately. I didn't even want to wait for a new position. I was delirious from pleasure and I couldn't believe how much sexual chemistry Curtis and I had together. Could sex always be this good between us?

Curtis caused my body to throb immensely until I wanted to beg him to release me from that feeling. I wanted to be fucked over and over again by that man. I would never need another bubble bath again as long as I had Curtis to help me relax.

He lifted me up into his arms and I gasped as I circled my arms around his neck. He plunged me down on his cock and my eyes rolled back into my head. His hands were underneath my ass and he used it as leverage to move me up and down on his cock.

I moved slowly with him, my body weakened from pleasure.

"Play with your pussy again Carrie, I want to see it. It was so hot the first time."

My eyes popped open. I smiled devilishly. I was sitting in his arms and my pussy was between us. He moved over to the kitchen wall and leaned my back against it.

"I want to see you please yourself; it turns me on and I'm going to fuck you really good while you do it."

I swirled my fingers around in my pussy juices before moving up to my clit, massaging it with my finger. I massaged into it closing my eyes as I enjoyed my own touch. He continued to rock me onto his cock so I was getting pleasure from that as well as my own doings. My eyes fluttered closed as I allowed all the pleasure to take complete control of me. I couldn't believe how sexy Curtis was; sexually it was like we were a perfect match. In fact when I opened my eyes he was staring down at my pussy, mesmerized by my movements. He looked up at me with fire in his eyes and the look on his face made me feel incredible. Like I was completely in control of his pleasure and I liked being in control. I loved the feeling of controlling his lust and I played with my pussy as I watched his cock slide in and out of me.

"That is so hot."

"I agree," I whispered.

I moaned as I pleasured myself, swirling my juices around my clit. I was throbbing all over and I desperately wanted to be fucked harder at that point.

"Please?"

"What are you asking for Carrie? What do you want; I will give you anything you want?"

"I want you. I want you to fuck me harder. Focus just on fucking me good Curtis."

"Oh I plan on doing just that sweetheart." He gripped my ass hard and moved me up and down him slowly and I gasped with how deep he went.

"Oh yes, this is nice. You're nice and tight baby. God your pussy feels so good." The level of deepness in that position was crazy good. He started moving a little faster and he just went deeper still.

I leaned my head back against the wall, delirious with pleasure. He fit inside me perfectly and I got a wave of pleasure every time he moved inside me. Curtis began pumping me a little faster, causing me to moan loudly. His cock was perfect and with the position we were using he was in the perfect spot to hit my G-spot over and over again. My body built up once again and I knew that he was going to cause me to cum all over his cock.

"Cum for me baby, I can see it on your face. Cum all over my cock baby."

I exploded then doing as he asked, screaming loudly. I was spent and yet he kept fucking me slowly. "Oh this feels so good Curtis. Wow, we will have to keep using this position."

"You have such a nice ass; you should feel what I have in my hands."

I giggled.

He slid inside my pussy hard. I cried out as pleasure over took my body. Curtis must have been exhausted from holding me up and yet he didn't say a word. I was on my back against the wall but he po- sitioned me so that his hands grasped under my ass and he lifted me up and supported my weight. My legs were still wrapped around his waist and I held on for dear life. I moaned, enjoying every inch of his cock as he pounded me over and over again. He kissed my breasts as he moved inside of me. I cried out realizing I had never experienced anything so sexy in my entire life. He pumped into me harder waves of pleasure rolling off of me. I smiled down at him and moaned loudly as another orgasm ripped through me. He was such a good lover that I was able to easily achieve multiple orgasms. Bonus!

"You have a real nice pussy Carrie. I like fucking you. You're perfect."

I moaned, loving the way he was making me feel, but even more so by the way he talked to me. Dirty talk won a lot of points with me. I just loved the way it sounded.

Curtis carried me back to the counter and laid me down again. He pulled out of my pussy and bent down for a kiss. He slid his fingers into my pussy and finger fucked me for a bit, he was making me wet all over again. "I want to take you from behind again baby, would you like that?"

"Very much so." I smiled and he pulled me up from the counter once again. He just wouldn't stop fucking me. Could he go all night? I was starting to think he could. Talk about a marathon lover. Maybe he was better than his own son.

I slid off the counter and I positioned myself so I had my back to him again and he slid his cock inside me.

"There we go darling; we are going to go easy. That feels good doesn't it?" I moaned in agreement.

"Okay, here we go, just stay relaxed. You feel incredible Carrie, you are nice and deep."

God, I had wanted Curtis so badly, he was all I ever thought about these days. I would probably always want him, he was such an incredible lover that I wanted to fuck him all night. I was so sexually satisfied but I could still just keep on going, I would have let him do just about anything to me. I was aching inside with want of him. Cleanup duty would be in order for sure after this romp. I hadn't realized the pleasure that could be brought to me by such a man. Curtis just wanted to bring as much pleasure to my body as I could stand and I was totally okay with that. He loved bringing me pleasure and I certainly loved taking it.

Curtis pumped his body against my ass and his cock was giving me such delicious sensations that spread all over my body.

"Oh yes baby, Carrie you feel so good."

He certainly felt huge when he was going in doggy-style. I felt full with him in my pussy, but I loved every moment of it. He then began to move his hips and meet my thrusts onto his cock. I thrust back against him and he went even deeper. I moaned as he picked up the pace, his smooth cock gliding inside and out.

"Are you okay Baby?"

"Yes," I whispered. "I couldn't be any better. You fuck so good Curtis."

"I love hearing that sweetheart."

"Keep fucking me Curtis, don't stop."

He rocked into me slowly continuing to meet my thrusts. I started rocking into him faster letting the waves of pleasure crash into me repeatedly, not much break in between. I loved it; I couldn't get enough of that man. I wanted to have him every waking moment that I could. How could I ever be apart from that man, he was too good. The sex was just too good to ever pass up.

"Oh god," I moaned.

He reached around and felt for my pussy. He rubbed against my moist clit giving me some added pleasure while he moved his cock inside me.

"Okay baby, I'm going to fuck you really good."

I thought I would lose my mind with the words coming out of his mouth. He was sexy and experienced and he was showing me such pleasure.

The whole length of his cock slowly pushed inside me causing me to let out a slow and powerful moan. There were so many different feelings and sensations going through my body at that moment. I was lost in a sea of pleasure and I wanted to let go of another orgasm.

"Give it to me."

I heard him chuckle and he started pumping me as I thrust onto him. I was delirious with the pleasure he was giving me, I needed it, I needed him.

What I didn't expect was for my pussy to become so wet. I was dripping wet and I felt a buildup once again. I couldn't believe I was about to cum again. God, the thought was just too delicious.

"Curtis, it feels good, it really does feel so good. I need it baby."

"I know baby. It's amazing isn't it?"

"Yes," I gasped, "I'm coming again."

My whole body shuddered as I came. He continued pumping inside of me breaking all reason inside my mind. He was glorious; all of it was so incredible. The best sex of my life was happening on Curtis's kitchen counter. Whether that was a good thing or a bad thing I didn't care. As I felt myself build up for another orgasm, the shudders ripped through my body causing me to ache to scream his name.

"Oh Carrie, I'm ready too baby. I'm going to fill up your pussy with cum. Here it comes Carrie!"

I moaned loving how sexy he was with his dirty talk. He came inside of me and collapsed against my back, exhausted. He was finally spent.

Curtis slid slowly out of me, his cock wet from our lovemaking and I knew for certain that I was going to be very sore the next day. The sex however was well worth any pain I would feel the next day. Yes, it would have all been worth it. He dug around the kitchen and handed me a roll of paper towel.

I laughed.

"Sorry, it's all I have. I don't exactly plan for these things to happen in my kitchen." He said smiling.

"Uh-huh, sure you don't."

I cleaned myself off as best that I could and slipped into my thong. I slipped into my jeans as I watched him rummaging around for his clothes that had fallen to the floor. Everything was covered in flour and we looked ridiculous as we got dressed. We both had smiles plastered on our faces however so the flour was the least of our worries. Finding his clothes, he quickly slipped into underwear and jeans, pulling his t-shirt over his head.

"So, that was dessert, right?"

"You bet. Hell I would have dessert like that anytime you want."

"Oh me too, that was delicious." I giggled and he came to me and kissed me firmly on the lips.

I looked up at Curtis as I slid into my bra and put my t-shirt back on. Everything was a little more rumpled than I would have liked but hopefully no one would notice as it was dark outside. They would probably see the flour before they saw any wrinkles in my clothes. I couldn't wipe the grin off my face though, so maybe the whole world would know what I had been up to. My hands shook from the toll the orgasms took on my body. Curtis was watching me dress and when I looked up at him he smiled. He was so handsome and the look of him made me want to start all over again. Would I ever be able to get enough of that man or was it always going to be this way? God, I hoped it was.

I giggled as I pulled him in for another deep kiss.

"Are you leaving?" He asked.

I nodded though I was sad to have the sex end or to see Curtis gone at all. I wanted him around me always. But I knew that Jeff would send out a search party if he didn't already. I had to go sleep in my own bed and formulate a plan for what I wanted with my life. I just wasn't sure if I was willing to live by Jeff's rules anymore. My happiness mattered.

He spanked my ass softly and said, "Thank you for letting me spend so much time with that bottom of yours."

I laughed, "You, Curtis, are very welcome."

Chapter Twenty-Six

A few weeks later I found myself in the aisle way of a small town drug store. I had driven quite a distance to find an area where I wouldn't be recognized. It was important that no one see what I was about to purchase. I didn't want a scandal breaking out. Things were bad enough already. When I had returned that night to my home Jeff was surprisingly still there. We hadn't spoken though. To his credit he looked ashamed but it really didn't matter to me any longer. Things were just too far gone now. It was as if he had made his choice. There had been no statements of wrongdoing, nor did he tell me he intended on leaving Cassandra.

He didn't look in the mood to chat and neither did I. I had gone to bed alone and he had not followed me in. It was the first time we had both been home but had not slept in the same bed. It carried on like that for a few weeks. We were just two passing ships in the night. We never discussed Cassandra again and I had to assume that he was still seeing her. I had to start admitting to myself that he had fallen in love with Cassandra. It was the only other explanation for his behavior. I had to accept that fact. I didn't think that he would ever divorce me though I was sure that Cassandra must be putting pressure on him to do exactly that. I would have loved to have been a fly on the wall when he told her about our fight. He would have been furious at her for coming here the night before our wedding. Clearly not mad enough to leave her, however.

Whether or not Jeff was going to stay with Cassandra was the least of my worries. I had started to get worried during a sex act with Curtis when he had gripped my breasts gently but I found it really hurt. I realized then that I was a week late for my period. The thought had shocked me to the core but I knew it to be true. There had been small changes in my body the whole time I had just ignored it. I needed to get a test and at least confirm it. That was why I headed to another town to do so. I didn't want anyone to find out about my pregnancy any sooner than necessary. I snatched up a test and headed to the cashier.

***

I found myself in the bathroom sitting on the toilet with the lid closed. I couldn't stop staring at the test; both lines clearly visible. So I was pregnant. My first instinct was that I could not have the child. Hell, I didn't even know who the father was. Granted Jeff and I hadn't slept together much in the past few months but there were times we did. I would need to see a doctor to confirm the actual timing, hopefully then I would know. Could I keep the baby? I certainly had enough money to care for it even if I left Jeff. I would have to leave someone. I had no intention of raising a child in the mess we had made. Jeff would have to choose. But did I even want Jeff anymore. He had hurt me so much and pushed me away, right into the arms of another man.

I had to see Curtis. I fled my apartment and drove as fast as I could to his home. His car was thankfully in the driveway. I raced up the steps to see him, not even knocking before I went through the door.

I found him in his study and I stood there in the doorway waiting for him to see me. I didn't know what to say and I wasn't sure how he would react to my news. He looked up immediately and seeing that I was visibly upset he came to me.

"I'm pregnant." I just uttered the words unsure of what else to say.

Curtis looked me in the eyes and nodded. "Are you okay?"

"Yes. I just don't know what to do. How can I possibly bring a child into this awful mess?"

"Stay with me. I will take care of you. I'm falling in love with you Carrie."

Shocked I just stood there. He had never said anything like that to me before and I had never been sure if our affair was just a physical thing. It was then that I realized I had been falling for Curtis as well. He was a good man who genuinely cared about me. He was older, yes, but I knew he would always take care of me.

"What if it's not yours?" I hated saying the words but there was no point in dancing around the subject.

"I don't care. It will all work out sweetheart. I promise you."

182

I smiled up at him. "Make me feel good."

He grinned, "That would be my pleasure. You are so very beautiful Carrie."

I kissed him, my tongue sliding gently into his mouth and touching his tongue. Electricity hit me and I started to feel warm all over. Oh God, what was with this guy? He was just so incredible, I physically needed him all the time and he felt exactly the same way. I never thought I would feel like this with anyone other than Jeff, but being there at that moment made me wonder if Jeff and I had always been wrong. Maybe my father had been right the whole time. We weren't meant to be together, we had just forced the issue because we fell in love. But had Jeff never came into my life I would never have met Curtis.

I smiled up at him again my eyes watching Curtis intensely. "I would like you to touch me."

He groaned. "Baby, that's all I want to do. I want to have that sweet ass in my hands once again. You are so hot Carrie."

"Oh Curtis, that is so sexy, I love the way you talk to me."

I moved closer to him and rubbed the front of his pants pressing my hand against his cock. Thank, god I wore a dress that day. Talk about easy access. I kneaded hard against him until I felt him growing hard against me. He had already been plenty hard when I started and feeling him grow turned me on that much more. I could make him rock hard so easily. He groaned at my touch and his hands slowly went up my dress and grasped my ass.

"I was wondering if we could try something new." He whispered.

"New?" I laughed, "Everything is new with you Curtis, and do you realize we rarely have sex in an actual bed?"

He smiled, "I can't help it. I just want you immediately regardless of where we are. I don't want to wait to find a bed. That takes too long, when I want you, I can't wait."

I loved hearing the things he said to me; he was truly the perfect man for me. I just responded to him in every way. Every cell in my body was aware of Curtis. I longed to be close to him, near him in every way possible. Not only that, Curtis made me feel safe.

"I know how you feel," I giggled.

I moved over to his desk and bent over slightly. He could see the bottom of my ass cheeks and he could probably tell I wasn't wearing any panties. And just like that he was hard as a rock. Harder than I had ever seen him before.

"I don't even need to undress. It will be nice and easy Curtis." I bent over his desk completely presenting my ass in the air for him.

"Oh dear God baby, you want me to fuck you from behind? Right against my desk? You are so hot Carrie. I'm going to make you feel incredible."

My firm ass was there for him to take and he wanted to slip in from behind nice and deep, I could tell by the intense look on his face. He was so perfect for me. I couldn't take it, I wanted him to pound me hard from behind and make me say his name again and again.

"Fuck it; I want to see your whole body baby. Let's get that dress off right now."

I gasped as he unzipped the back of my dress and pulled it up over my head. I turned around and he looked down at my breasts.

My breasts though small were snug within my bra. I released them from the bra and they hung perky and round before him. My breasts were nice and round, waiting there for him to suck on. He lost all control and went to me.

I hoped that he was going to give me exactly what I wanted. He was going to fuck me good I just knew it. He squeezed my breasts, his mouth finding my nipple and sucking on it hard. I released a soft cry and he nipped me with his teeth.

Curtis sucked on my breast while his fingers found my opening. He loved how I was always ready for him, my pussy wet with need for him. "Oh baby, you are already so wet."

184

He plunged a finger inside me and fucked me gently while I mewed in his arms. I was his heroin and he needed to fuck me more than anything. I felt exactly the same way, Curtis was my drug and I needed him daily. He caused me to forget all sense of reasoning and the fog that surrounded us when he was around was all that mattered. I wanted him and I was going to get him. He lifted me up and set me atop his desk.

"Don't worry sweetheart, I'm going to fuck you good doggy. I just want something first."

I lie back onto the wooden desk and spread my legs with my high heels on the edge of the desk. Seeing me spread out like that before him made Curtis want to fuck me right then but he had something better in mind. That much was obvious. He pulled his office chair around and set it before me. He sat down and bent forward placing his lips on my clit. I gasped in surprise as his lips touched my pussy. He loved tasting me and drank me in as I came against his mouth. It was terribly hard to keep quiet while he was providing my body with such exquisite pleasure.

He licked me like I was ice cream and plunged his tongue inside me. I ached to be fucked but having him taste me was hard to pass up. He licked my pussy all over, having me cum in his mouth made him so horny.

"Baby, you are so hot, I love this."

I writhed against him and he knew he had to have me. I couldn't believe we were fucking right there in his office, where anyone could walk in and see us. But at least it was his home office so it was less likely that would happen. The fact that it was his office however made it so much more exciting.

So much for the quickie fuck but things with Curtis and I always had to be right and perfect. There was no need to rush great sex.

He pulled me up to him and I hopped off the desk. I turned around and leaning forward against the desk, my firm ass high in the air Curtis slid inside my warm pussy and felt the deepness. He groaned with pleasure, and I felt amazing and I doubted that I would ever tire of having him inside me. He was so deep I couldn't believe how incredible I felt.

"Harder Curtis, please."

That was all it took, despite the fact that we were fucking in his office, he pumped against me hard feeling every inch of me. My fingers clenched against the desk as waves of pleasure went through me. I really had to hold back from not screaming his name. There was going to come a time when I wouldn't be able to take his cock so deep so I wanted to feel him as much as I could then.

I would be sore tomorrow; he was guaranteeing that much. He fucked me hard, listening to me whisper his name. The moment became more intense and I screamed out his name. He pumped me harder while he reached over and rubbed my clit, I was so wet that his fingers slide over my pussy very easily. He bent forward and kissed my shoulder, nipping it gently. He fondled my breasts from underneath. He could feel me tightening around him and he knew I was going to cum again. He pumped faster and I muffled my cries of pleasure against my palms. Oh he was good, really good. My orgasm broke through and I whimpered as I finished. He continued to pump me hard until he wasn't ready to give up yet.

"Oh Curtis, I can't stop thinking about you inside me. I just had to have you. And it's my turn to make you feel better."

Curtis smiled, loving the way I talked to him. When I talked dirty it drove him wild, we were kindred spirits.

Curtis went to lift me up onto his cock when I stopped him. I backed him up to his office chair and pushed him down. He laughed, enjoying the look on my face. I had the power now and I was enjoying every bit of it. He looked me up from top to bottom, resting his eyes finally on my perfectly waxed pussy. His cock grew hard and ready and I knew he didn't want to wait any longer. I climbed on top of him in that chair and kissed him passionately, his hands on my breasts.

I was about to blow his mind. "You want to cum inside me so badly, don't you baby?"

186

"God yes Carrie, I want to feel inside your pussy so badly."

My kisses went from his mouth to his jawline, nipping the side. I trailed kisses down his chest and licked the trail that led to his throbbing cock. I slid down the chair wanting his cock once again. He was just going to have to wait a bit longer. The torture would be worth it.

I licked and sucked the tip of his cock teasingly. "You little devil you."

I lapped at his cock while looking him straight in the eyes. He was slowly losing his mind; it wasn't hard to figure out. I quickly climbed on his lap once again and moved above him, plunging his cock inside me. I gasped above him and he groaned in pleasure. Curtis watched as I rode him slowly moving on his cock with tortuously slow rhythm. My breasts bounced above him and he had the best view in the house. My hair fell over my breasts as I bounced on his cock. He put his hands on my hips and grinded me onto him. I moaned in the kitten-like way that drove him half mad. I tightened around his cock and he knew I was about to come around him. I came quite vocally and he laughed with joy.

I smiled down at him while I rode him, I took his hand and sucked on his middle finger while I rode him hard. "Wow baby, that is so hot."

I began to ride his cock harder, my body grinding into his. The tension inside was building and he was going to blow with me while I was in complete control over his orgasm. "Oh god Carrie, that feels so good." He came inside me hard and I rocked onto him continuously causing him to have the most intense orgasm.

He was spent and I felt wondrous with me on top of him. I bent forward and licked his mouth before kissing him hard. I climbed off and opened up a drawer to grab some Kleenex to clean off. Being with Curtis had been amazing...both times. It felt glorious having him inside me. I could smell his cologne around us and I climbed on his lap again and held him closer to me.

"You smell fantastic Curtis."

He laughed, "So do you sweetheart."

Chapter Twenty-Seven

I returned home that day to talk to Jeff. I had sent him a text message earlier in the day telling him that we needed to talk and that I would expect him to be home that evening. I would normally have gone to open a bottle of wine but things had changed. I decided to put on some tea instead while I waited for him.

It wasn't long before he came through the door and found me in the kitchen drinking tea. He sat down across from me and looked at me with sad eyes. It seemed like forever since I had really looked at him. I had loved him so much and now it seemed as if I was staring at a stranger. What had happened to us?

"Are you asking me for a divorce?" He asked simply.

"Yes."

"Because of Cassandra?"

Just hearing her name was like a hot poker going into my chest. "I have other reasons but that's a good start."

"I'm sorry Carrie. I never meant to hurt you. Believe it or not I don't want to lose you. Maybe I can make some changes, put you first, spend less time with Cassandra."

I almost laughed, "Or you could leave her entirely."

He looked down at the table. "I can't do that."

"Why? Because you love her?"

He didn't look back up so I forged ahead. "I'm pregnant Jeff and I want a divorce. I've met someone and I would like to pursue things further with him."

"But that's my baby."

"Actually it may not be."

His face hardened, "I guess I can hardly be mad at you after what I have done. I just wasn't aware that you were seeing anyone else."

"Of course not," I said bitterly. "But you may be a little upset to find out it's your father."

He stared at me stunned, "No."

"Yes. I love him Jeff. I can't bring a child into this three ring circus and I think Cassandra probably wants you all to herself anyways. Though I doubt she will ever be able to trust you. The rest doesn't matter. Goodbye."

I got up from the table and I left the room without another word. I didn't want to argue or hurl blame around. I wanted to go back to the home where there was a man who wanted to love me forever.

###

www.ingramcontent.com/pod-product-compliance
Lightning Source LLC
Chambersburg PA
CBHW072136170626
46813CB00004BA/1586